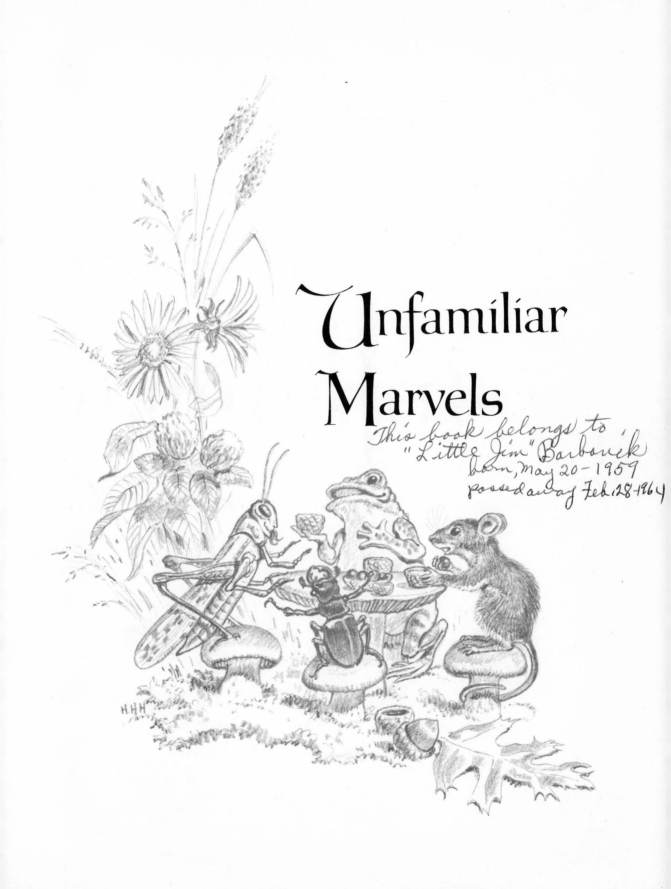

Unfamiliar Marvels

VOLUME 6

THE
GOLDEN TREASURY
OF
CHILDREN'S LITERATURE

EDITED AND SELECTED

ILLUSTRATED BY

HANS HELWEG

ALEXANDER JAMES

DENVER GILLEN

GORDON LAITE

JEAN WINSLOW

FRANK DANIEL

ROBERT J. LEE

LILIAN OBLIGADO

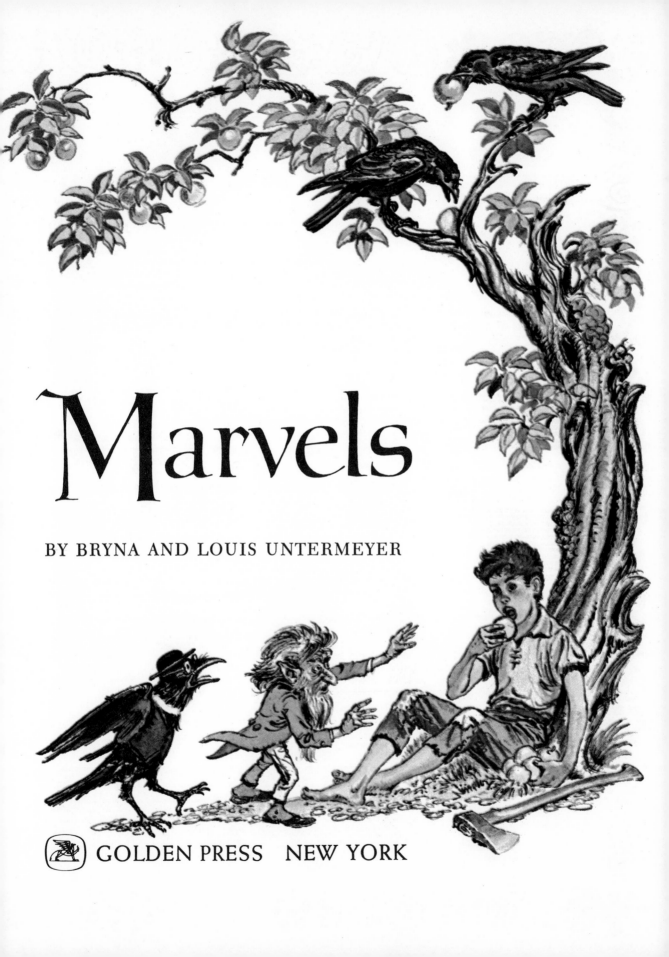

Marvels

BY BRYNA AND LOUIS UNTERMEYER

GOLDEN PRESS   NEW YORK

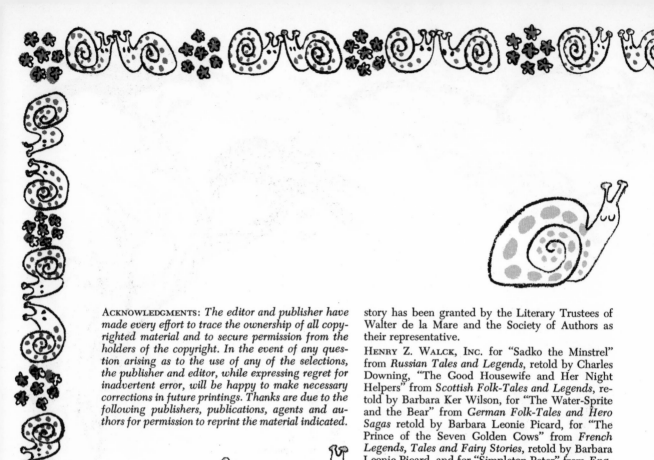

ACKNOWLEDGMENTS: *The editor and publisher have made every effort to trace the ownership of all copyrighted material and to secure permission from the holders of the copyright. In the event of any question arising as to the use of any of the selections, the publisher and editor, while expressing regret for inadvertent error, will be happy to make necessary corrections in future printings. Thanks are due to the following publishers, publications, agents and authors for permission to reprint the material indicated.*

THE BODLEY HEAD LTD. for "The Reluctant Dragon" from *Dream Days* by Kenneth Grahame.

PADRAIC COLUM for "The Man with the Bag" from *The Big Tree of Bunlahy*, published by permission of the author.

THE CRESSETT PRESS for "A Meal with a Magician" from *My Friend Mr. Leakey* by J. B. S. Haldane.

LONGMANS, GREEN AND COMPANY for "The Language of Beasts" and "To Your Good Health!" from *The Crimson Fairy Book* by Andrew Lang, for "The Thanksgiving of the Wazir" and "Grasp All, Lose All" from *The Olive Fairy Book* by Andrew Lang.

THE SOCIETY OF AUTHORS for "The Dutch Cheese" by Walter de la Mare. Permission to include the story has been granted by the Literary Trustees of Walter de la Mare and the Society of Authors as their representative.

HENRY Z. WALCK, INC. for "Sadko the Minstrel" from *Russian Tales and Legends*, retold by Charles Downing, "The Good Housewife and Her Night Helpers" from *Scottish Folk-Tales and Legends*, retold by Barbara Ker Wilson, for "The Water-Sprite and the Bear" from *German Folk-Tales and Hero Sagas* retold by Barbara Leonie Picard, for "The Prince of the Seven Golden Cows" from *French Legends, Tales and Fairy Stories*, retold by Barbara Leonie Picard, and for "Simpleton Peter" from *English Fables and Fairy Stories*, retold by James Reeves. Reprinted by permission of the publisher and the authors.

LOUIS UNTERMEYER for the adaptation of "Count Beet."

The editors acknowledge with thanks the painstaking assistance of Millie Isaacs in the preparation of the manuscript.

Decoration by KATHY KELM

CONTENTS

FOREWORD

Here come more revelations, surprises, magics and marvels.
Many of them are little known;
some of them have never crossed the Atlantic;
one of them is so new that it has never before
appeared in print.
You will meet a magician who lives in modern London
and has an octopus for a servant;
a giant who is so petty that he puts up
a "No Trespassing" sign on his garden wall;
a water-sprite who is dissatisfied with his stream
and moves into a house;
a boy who draws nothing but pictures of cats
with the most astonishing results;
a shepherd who demands a princess as his price
for obeying a king;
a prehistoric gnome who tries to make
friends with men and fails to understand them.
Perhaps the most surprising tale of all is
the first one in this section.
One usually thinks of dragons as fierce, fire-breathing,
dagger-clawed, scaly, implacable monsters.
But Kenneth Grahame, author of The Wind in the Willows,
pictures a dragon who is placid, dreamy, writes poetry,
and firmly refuses to fight anyone or anything.

The Reluctant Dragon

From Dream Days

BY KENNETH GRAHAME
Illustrated by ALEXANDER JAMES

LONG AGO—might have been hundreds of years ago—in a cottage half-way between this village and yonder shoulder of the Downs up there, a shepherd lived with his wife and their little son. Now the shepherd spent his days—and at certain times of the year his nights too—up on the wide ocean-bosom of the Downs, with only the sun and the stars and the sheep for company, and the friendly chattering world of men and women far out of sight and hearing. But his little son, when he wasn't helping his father, and often when he was as well, spent much of his time buried in big volumes that he borrowed from the affable gentry and interested parsons of the country round about. And his parents were very fond of him, and rather proud

of him too, though they didn't let on in his hearing, so he was left to go his own way and read as much as he liked; and instead of frequently getting a cuff on the side of the head, as might very well have happened to him, he was treated more or less as an equal by his parents, who sensibly thought it a very fair division of labour that they should supply the practical knowledge, and he the book-learning. They knew that book-learning often came in useful at a pinch, in spite of what their neighbours said. What the Boy chiefly dabbled in was natural history and fairy-tales, and he just took them as they came, in a sandwichy sort of way, without making any distinctions; and really his course of reading strikes one as rather sensible:

12

One evening the shepherd, who for some nights past had been disturbed and preoccupied, and off his usual mental balance, came home all of a tremble, and, sitting down at the table where his wife and son were peacefully employed, she with her seam, he in following out the adventures of the Giant with no Heart in his Body, exclaimed with much agitation:

"It's all up with me, Maria! Never no more can I go up on them there Downs, was it ever so!"

"Now don't you take on like that," said his wife, who was a *very* sensible woman: "but tell us all about it first, whatever it is as has given you this shake-up, and then me and you and the son here, between us, we ought to be able to get to the bottom of it!"

"It began some nights ago," said the shepherd. "You know that cave up there —I never liked it, somehow, and the sheep never liked it neither, and when sheep don't like a thing there's generally some reason for it. Well, for some time past there's been faint noises coming from that cave—noises like heavy sighings, with grunts mixed up in them; and sometimes a snoring, far away down— *real* snoring, yet somehow not *honest* snoring, like you and me o' nights, you know!"

"*I* know," remarked the Boy quietly.

"Of course I was terrible frightened," the shepherd went on; "yet somehow I couldn't keep away. So this very evening, before I come down, I took a cast round by the cave, quietly. And, there—O Lord! there I saw him at last, as plain as I see you!"

"Saw *who*?" said his wife, beginning to share in her husband's nervous terror.

"Why *him*, I'm a-telling you!" said the shepherd. "He was sticking half-way out of the cave, and seemed to be enjoying of the cool of the evening in a poetical sort of way. He was as big as four cart-horses, and all covered with shiny scales —deep-blue scales at the top of him, shading off to a tender sort o' green below. As he breathed, there was a sort of flicker over his nostrils that you see over our chalk roads on a baking windless day in summer. He had his chin on his paws, and I should say he was meditating about things. Oh, yes, a peaceable sort o' beast enough, and not ramping or carrying on or doing anything but what was quite right and proper. I admit all that. And yet, what am I to do? Scales, you know, and claws, and a tail for certain, though I didn't see that end of him —I ain't *used* to 'em, and I don't *hold* with 'em, and that's a fact!"

The Boy, who had apparently been absorbed in his book during his father's recital, now closed the volume, yawned, clasped his hands behind his head, and said sleepily: "It's all right, father. Don't you worry. It's only a dragon."

"Only a dragon?" cried his father. "What do you mean, sitting there, you and your dragons? *Only* a dragon indeed! And what do *you* know about it?"

" 'Cos it *is*, and 'cos I *do* know," replied the Boy quietly. "Look here, father, you know we've each of us got our line. *You* know about sheep, and weather, and things; *I* know about dragons. I always said, you know, that that cave up there was a dragon-cave. I always said it must have belonged to a dragon some time, and ought to belong

13

to a dragon now, if rules count for anything. Well, now you tell me it *has* got
a dragon, and so *that's* all right. I'm not
half as much surprised as when you told
me it *hadn't* got a dragon. Rules always
come right if you wait quietly. Now,
please, just leave this all to me. And I'll

stroll up to-morrow morning—no, in the
morning I can't, I've got a whole heap of
things to do—well, perhaps in the evening, if I'm quite free, I'll go up and have
a talk to him, and you'll find it'll be all
right. Only please, don't you go worrying
round there without me. You don't

15

understand 'em a bit, and they're very sensitive, you know!"

"He's quite right, father," said the sensible mother. "As he says, dragons is his line and not ours. He's wonderful knowing about book-beasts, as everyone allows. And to tell the truth, I'm not half happy in my own mind, thinking of that poor animal lying alone up there, without a bit o' hot supper or anyone to change the news with; and maybe we'll be able to do something for him; and if he ain't quite respectable our Boy'll find it out quick enough. He's got a pleasant sort o' way with him that makes everybody tell him everything."

Next day, after he'd had his tea, the Boy strolled up the chalky track that led to the summit of the Downs; and there, sure enough, he found the dragon, stretched lazily on the sward in front of his cave. The view from that point was a magnificent one. To the right and left, the bare and billowy leagues of Downs; in front, the vale, with its clustered homesteads, its threads of white roads running through orchards and well-tilled acreage, and, far away, a hint of grey old cities on the horizon. A cool breeze played over the surface of the grass, and the silver shoulder of a large moon was showing above distant junipers. No wonder the dragon seemed in a peaceful and contented mood; indeed, as the Boy approached he could hear the beast purring with a happy regularity. "Well, we live and learn!" he said to himself. "None of my books ever told me that dragons purred!"

"Hullo, dragon!" said the Boy quietly, when he had got up to him.

The dragon, on hearing the approaching footsteps, made the beginning of a courteous effort to rise. But when he saw it was a Boy, he set his eyebrows severely.

"Now don't you hit me," he said; "or bung stones, or squirt water, or anything. I won't have it, I tell you!"

"Not goin' to hit you," said the Boy wearily, dropping on the grass beside the beast: "and don't, for goodness' sake, keep on saying 'Don't'; I hear so much of it, and it's monotonous, and makes me tired. I've simply looked in to ask you how you were and all that sort of thing; but if I'm in the way I can easily clear out. I've lots of friends, and no one can say I'm in the habit of shoving myself in where I'm not wanted!"

"No, no, don't go off in a huff," said the dragon hastily; "fact is—I'm as happy up here as the day's long; never without an occupation, dear fellow, never without an occupation! And yet, between ourselves, it is a trifle dull at times."

The Boy bit off a stalk of grass and chewed it. "Going to make a long stay here?" he asked politely.

"Can't hardly say at present," replied the dragon. "It seems a nice place enough—but I've only been here a short time, and one must look about and reflect and consider before settling down. It's rather a serious thing, settling down. Besides—now I'm going to tell you something! You'd never guess it if you tried ever so!—fact is, I'm such a confoundedly lazy beggar!"

"You surprise me," said the Boy civilly.

"It's the sad truth," the dragon went on, settling down between his paws and evidently delighted to have found a listener at last: "and I fancy that's really how I came to be here. You see, all the other fellows were so active and *earnest* and all that sort of thing—always rampaging, and skirmishing, and scouring the desert sands, and pacing the margin of the sea, and chasing knights all over the place, and devouring damsels, and going on generally—whereas I liked to get my meals regular and then to prop my back against a bit of rock and snooze a bit, and wake up and think of things going on and how they kept going on just the same, you know! So when it happened I got fairly caught."

"When *what* happened, please?" asked the Boy.

"That's just what I don't precisely know," said the dragon. "I suppose the earth sneezed, or shook itself, or the bottom dropped out of something. Anyhow there was a shake and a roar and a general stramash, and I found myself miles away underground and wedged in as tight as tight. Well, thank goodness, my wants are few, and at any rate I had peace and quietness and wasn't always being asked to come along and *do* something. And I've got such an active mind—always occupied, I assure you! But time went on, and there was a certain sameness about the life, and at last I began to think it would be fun to work my way upstairs and see what you other fellows were doing. So I scratched and burrowed, and worked this way and that way, and at last I came out through this cave here. And I like the country, and the view, and the people—what I've seen of 'em—and on the whole I feel inclined to settle down here."

"What's your mind always occupied about?" asked the Boy.

The dragon coloured slightly and looked away. Presently he said bashfully:

"Did you ever—just for fun—try to make up poetry—verses, you know?"

" 'Course I have," said the Boy. "Heaps of it. And some of it's quite good, I feel sure, only there's no one here cares about it. Mother's very kind and all that, when I read it to her, and so's father for that matter. But somehow they don't seem to ——"

"Exactly," cried the dragon; "my own case, exactly. They don't seem to, and you can't argue with 'em about it. Now you've got culture, you have, I could tell it on you at once, and I should just like your candid opinion about some little things I threw off lightly, when I was down there. I'm awfully pleased to have met you, and I'm hoping the other neighbours will be equally agreeable. There was a very nice old gentleman up here only last night, but he didn't seem to want to intrude."

"That was my father," said the boy, "and he *is* a nice old gentleman, and I'll introduce you some day if you like."

"Can't you two come up here and dine or something to-morrow?" asked the dragon eagerly. "Only, of course, if you've got nothing better to do," he added quite politely.

"Thanks awfully," said the Boy, "but we don't go out anywhere without my mother, and, to tell you the truth, I'm afraid she mightn't quite approve of you. You see, there's no getting over the hard fact that you're a dragon, is there? And when you talk of settling down, and the neighbours, and so on, I can't help feeling that you don't quite realize your

position. You're an enemy of the human race, you see!"

"Haven't got an enemy in the world," said the dragon cheerfully. "Too lazy to make 'em, to begin with. And if I *do* read other fellows my poetry, I'm always ready to listen to theirs!"

"Oh, dear!" cried the boy, "I wish you'd try and grasp the situation properly. When the other people find you out, they'll come after you with spears and swords and all sorts of things. You'll have to be exterminated, according to their way of looking at it! You're a scourge, and a pest, and a baneful monster!"

"Not a word of truth in it," said the dragon, wagging his head solemnly. "Character'll bear the strictest investigation. And now, there's a little sonnet-thing I was working on when you appeared on the scene——"

"Oh, if you *won't* be sensible," cried the Boy, getting up, "I'm going off home. No, I can't stop for sonnets; my mother's sitting up. I'll look you up to-morrow, sometime or other, and do for goodness' sake try and realize that you're a pestilential scourge, or you'll find yourself in a most awful fix. Good night!"

The Boy found it an easy matter to set the mind of his parents at ease about his new friend. They had always left that branch to him, and they took his word without a murmur. The shepherd was formally introduced and many compliments and kind enquiries were exchanged. His wife, however, though expressing her willingness to do anything she could—to mend things, or set the cave to rights, or cook a little something when the dragon had been poring over sonnets and forgotten his meals, as male

things *will* do—could not be brought to recognize him formally. The fact that he was a dragon and "they didn't know who he was" seemed to count for everything with her. She made no objection, however, to her little son spending his evenings with the dragon quietly, so long as he was home by nine o'clock: and many a pleasant night they had, sitting on the sward, while the dragon told stories of old, old times, when dragons were quite plentiful and the world was a livelier place than it is now, and life was full of thrills and jumps and surprises.

What the Boy had feared, however, soon came to pass. The most modest and retiring dragon in the world, if he's as big as four cart-horses and covered with blue scales, cannot keep altogether out of the public view. And so in the village tavern of nights the fact that a real live dragon sat brooding in the cave on the Downs was naturally a subject for talk. Though the villagers were extremely frightened, they were rather proud as well. It was a distinction to have a dragon of your own, and it was felt to be a feather in the cap of the village. Still, all were agreed that this sort of thing couldn't be allowed to go on. The dreadful beast must be exterminated, the countryside must be freed from this pest, this terror, this destroying scourge. The fact that not even a hen-roost was the worse for the dragon's arrival wasn't allowed to have anything to do with it. He was a dragon, and he couldn't deny it, and if he didn't choose to behave as such that was his own look-out. But in spite of much valiant talk no hero was found willing to take sword and spear

and free the suffering village and win deathless fame; and each night's heated discussion always ended in nothing. Meanwhile the dragon, a happy Bohemian, lolled on the turf, enjoyed the sunsets, told antediluvian anecdotes to the Boy, and polished his old verses while meditating on fresh ones.

One day the Boy, on walking into the village, found everything wearing a festal appearance which was not to be accounted for in the calendar. Carpets and gay-coloured stuffs were hung out of the windows, the church-bells clamoured noisily, the little street was flower-strewn, and the whole population jostled each other along either side of it, chattering, shoving, and ordering each other to stand back. The Boy saw a friend of his own age in the crowd and hailed him.

"What's up?" he cried. "Is it the players, or bears, or a circus, or what?"

"It's all right," his friend hailed back. "He's a-coming."

"*Who's* a-coming?" demanded the Boy, thrusting into the throng.

"Why, St. George, of course," replied his friend. "He's heard tell of our dragon, and he's comin' on purpose to slay the deadly beast, and free us from his horrid yoke. O my! won't there be a jolly fight!"

Here was news indeed! The Boy felt that he ought to make quite sure for himself, and he wriggled himself in between the legs of his good-natured elders, abusing them all the time for their unmannerly habit of shoving. Once in the front rank, he breathlessly awaited the arrival.

Presently from the far-away end of the line came the sound of cheering. Next, the measured tramp of a great war-horse made his heart beat quicker, and then he found himself cheering with the rest, as, amidst welcoming shouts, shrill cries of women, uplifting of babies, and waving of handkerchiefs, St. George paced slowly up the street. The Boy's heart stood still and he breathed with sobs, the beauty and the grace of the hero were so far beyond anything he had yet seen. His fluted armour was inlaid with gold, his plumed helmet hung at his saddle-bow, and his thick fair hair framed a face gracious and gentle beyond expression till you caught the sternness in his eyes. He drew rein in front of the little inn, and the villagers crowded round with greetings and thanks and voluble statements of their wrongs and grievances and oppressions. The Boy heard the grave gentle voice of the Saint, assuring them that all would be well now, and that he would stand by them and see them righted and free them from their foe; then he dismounted and passed through the doorway and the crowd poured in after him. But the Boy made off up the hill as fast as he could lay his legs to the ground.

"It's all up, dragon!" he shouted as soon as he was within sight of the beast. "He's coming! He's here now! You'll have to pull yourself together and *do* something at last!"

The dragon was licking his scales and rubbing them with a bit of house-flannel the Boy's mother had lent him, till he shone like a great turquoise.

"Don't be *violent*, Boy," he said without looking round. "Sit down and get your breath, and try and remember that the noun governs the verb, and then perhaps you'll be good enough to tell me *who's* coming?"

"That's right, take it coolly," said the Boy. "Hope you'll be half as cool when I've got through with my news. It's only St. George who's coming, that's all; he

rode into the village half an hour ago. Of course you can lick him—a great big fellow like you! But I thought I'd warn you, 'cos he's sure to be round early, and he's got the longest, wickedest-looking spear you ever did see!" And the Boy got up and began to jump round in sheer delight at the prospect of the battle.

"O deary, deary me," moaned the dragon; "this is too awful. I won't see him, and that's flat. I don't want to know the fellow at all. I'm sure he's not nice. You must tell him to go away at once, please. Say he can write if he likes, but I can't give him an interview. I'm not seeing anybody at present."

"Now, dragon, dragon," said the Boy imploringly, "don't be perverse and wrong-headed. You've *got* to fight him some time or other, you know, 'cos he's St. George and you're the dragon. Better get it over and then we can go on with the sonnets. And you ought to consider other people a little, too. If it's been dull up here for you, think how dull it's been for me!"

"My dear little man," said the dragon solemnly, "just understand, once for all, that I can't fight and I won't fight. I've never fought in my life, and I'm not going to begin now, just to give you a Roman holiday. In old days I always let the other fellows—the *earnest* fellows—do all the fighting, and no doubt that's why I have the pleasure of being here now."

"But if you don't fight he'll cut your head off!" gasped the Boy, miserable at the prospect of losing both his fight and his friend.

"Oh, I think not," said the dragon in his lazy way. "You'll be able to arrange something. I've every confidence in you, you're such a *manager*. Just run down, there's a dear chap, and make it all right. I leave it entirely to you."

The Boy made his way back to the village in a state of great despondency. First of all, there wasn't going to be any fight; next, his dear and honoured friend the dragon hadn't shown up in quite such a heroic light as he would have liked; and lastly, whether the dragon was a hero at heart or not, it made no difference, for St. George would most undoubtedly cut his head off. "Arrange things indeed!" he said bitterly to himself. "The dragon treats the whole affair as if it was an invitation to tea and croquet."

The villagers were straggling homewards as he passed up the street, all of them in the highest spirits, and gleefully discussing the splendid fight that was in store.

The Boy pursued his way to the inn, and passed into the principal chamber, where St. George now sat alone, musing over the chances of the fight, and the sad stories of rapine and of wrong that had so lately been poured into his sympathetic ears.

"May I come in, St. George?" said the Boy politely, as he paused at the door. "I want to talk to you about this little matter of the dragon, if you're not tired of it by this time."

"Yes, come in, Boy," said the Saint kindly. "Another tale of misery and wrong, I fear me. Is it a kind parent, then, of whom the tyrant has bereft you? Or some tender sister or brother? Well, it shall soon be avenged."

"Nothing of the sort," said the Boy.

"There's a misunderstanding somewhere, and I want to put it right. The fact is, this is a *good* dragon."

"Exactly," said St. George, smiling pleasantly, "I quite understand. A good *dragon*. Believe me, I do not in the least regret that he is an adversary worthy of my steel, and no feeble specimen of his noxious tribe."

"But he's *not* a noxious tribe," cried the Boy distressedly. "Oh dear, oh dear, how *stupid* men are when they get an idea into their heads! I tell you he's a *good* dragon, and a friend of mine, and tells me the most beautiful stories you ever heard, all about old times and when he was little. And he's been so kind to mother, and mother'd do anything for him. And father likes him too, though father doesn't hold with art and poetry much, and always falls asleep when the dragon starts talking about *style*. But the fact is, nobody can help liking him when once they know him. He's so engaging and so trustful, and as simple as a child!"

"Sit down, and draw your chair up," said St. George. "I like a fellow who sticks up for his friends, and I'm sure the dragon has his good points, if he's got a friend like you. But that's not the question. All this evening I've been listening, with grief and anguish unspeakable, to tales of murder, theft, and wrong; rather too highly coloured, perhaps, not always quite convincing, but forming in the main a most serious roll of crime. History teaches us that the greatest rascals often possess all the domestic virtues; and I fear that your cultivated friend, in spite of the qualities which have won (and rightly) your regard, has got to be speedily exterminated."

"Oh, you've been taking in all the yarns those fellows have been telling you," said the Boy impatiently. "Why, our villagers are the biggest story-tellers in all the country round. It's a known fact. You're a stranger in these parts, or else you'd have heard it already. All they want is a *fight*. They're the most awful beggars for getting up fights—it's meat and drink to them. Dogs, bulls, dragons —anything so long as it's a fight. Why, they've got a poor innocent badger in the stable behind here, at this moment. They were going to have some fun with him to-day, but they're saving him up now till *your* little affair's over. And I've no doubt they've been telling you what a hero you were, and how you were bound to win, in the cause of right and justice, and so on; but let me tell you, I came down the street just now, and they were betting six to four on the dragon freely!"

"Six to four on the dragon!" murmured St. George sadly, resting his cheek on his hand. "This is an evil world, and sometimes I begin to think that all the wickedness in it is not entirely bottled up inside the dragons. And yet—may not this wily beast have misled you as to his real character, in order that your good report of him may serve as a cloak for his evil deeds? Nay, may there not be, at this very moment, some hapless Princess immured within yonder gloomy cavern?"

The moment he had spoken, St. George was sorry for what he had said, the Boy looked so genuinely distressed.

"I assure you, St. George," he said earnestly, "there's nothing of the sort in the cave at all. The dragon's a real gentleman, every inch of him, and I may say that no one would be more shocked and grieved than he would, at hearing you talk in that—that *loose* way about matters on which he has very strong views!"

"Well, perhaps I've been over-credulous," said St. George. "Perhaps I've misjudged the animal. But what are we to do? Here are the dragon and I, almost face to face, each supposed to be thirsting for each other's blood. I don't see any way out of it, exactly. What do you suggest? Can't you arrange things, somehow?"

"That's just what the dragon said," replied the Boy, rather nettled. "Really, the way you two seem to leave everything to me—I suppose you couldn't be persuaded to go away quietly, could you?"

"Impossible, I fear," said the Saint. "Quite against the rules. *You* know that as well as I do."

"Well, then, look here," said the Boy, "it's early yet—would you mind strolling up with me and seeing the dragon and talking it over? It's not far, and any friend of mine will be most welcome."

"Well, it's *irregular*," said St. George, rising, "but really it seems about the most sensible thing to do. You're taking a lot of trouble on your friend's account," he added good-naturedly, as they passed out through the door together. "But cheer up! Perhaps there won't have to be any fight after all."

"Oh, but I hope there will, though!" replied the little fellow wistfully.

"I've brought a friend to see you, dragon," said the Boy rather loud.

The dragon woke up with a start. "I was just—er—thinking about things," he

said in his simple way. "Very pleased to make your acquaintance, sir. Charming weather we're having!"

"This is St. George," said the Boy shortly. "St. George, let me introduce you to the dragon. We've come up to talk things over quietly, dragon, and now for goodness' sake do let us have a little straight common sense, and come to some practical business-like arrangement, for I'm sick of views and theories of life and personal tendencies, and all that sort of thing. I may perhaps add that my mother's sitting up."

"So glad to meet you, St. George," began the dragon rather nervously, "because you've been a great traveller, I hear, and I've always been rather a stay-

24

at-home. But I can show you many antiquities, many interesting features of our countryside, if you're stopping here any time——"

"I think," said St. George in his frank, pleasant way, "that we'd really better take the advice of our young friend here, and try to come to some understanding, on a business footing, about this little affair of ours. Now don't you think that after all the simplest plan would be just to fight it out, according to the rules, and let the best man win? They're betting on you, I may tell you, down in the village, but I don't mind that!"

"Oh, yes, *do*, dragon," said the Boy delightedly; "it'll save such a lot of bother!"

"My young friend, you shut up," said the dragon severely. "Believe me, St. George," he went on, "there's nobody in the world I'd sooner oblige than you and this young gentleman here. But the whole thing's nonsense, and conventionality, and popular thick-headedness. There's absolutely nothing to fight about, from beginning to end. And anyhow I'm not going to, so that settles it!"

"But supposing I make you?" said St. George, rather nettled.

"You can't," said the dragon triumphantly. "I should only go into my cave and retire for a time down the hole I came up. You'd soon get heartily sick of sitting outside and waiting for me to come out and fight you. And as soon as you'd really gone away, why, I'd come up again gaily, for I tell you frankly, I like this place, and I'm going to stay here!"

St. George gazed for a while on the fair landscape around them. "But this would be a beautiful place for a fight," he began again persuasively. "These great bare rolling Downs for the arena —and me in my golden armour showing up against your big blue scaly coils! Think what a picture it would make!"

"Now you're trying to get at me through my artistic sensibilities," said the dragon. "But it won't work. Not but what it would make a very pretty picture, as you say," he added, wavering a little.

"We seem to be getting rather nearer to *business*," put in the Boy. "You must see, dragon, that there's got to be a fight of some sort, 'cos you can't want to have to go down that dirty old hole again and stop there till goodness knows when."

"It might be arranged," said St. George thoughtfully. "I *must* spear you somewhere, of course, but I'm not bound to hurt you very much. There's such a lot of you that there must be a few *spare* places somewhere. Here, for instance, just behind your foreleg. It couldn't hurt you much, just here!"

"Now you're tickling, George," said the dragon coyly. "No, that place won't do at all. Even if it didn't hurt—and I'm sure it would, awfully—it would make me laugh, and that would spoil everything."

"Let's try somewhere else, then," said St. George patiently. "Under your neck, for instance—all these folds of thick skin—if I speared you here you'd never even know I'd done it!"

"Yes, but are you sure you can hit off the right place?" asked the dragon anxiously.

"Of course I am," said St. George, with confidence. "You leave that to me!"

"It's just because I've *got* to leave it to you that I'm asking," replied the dragon rather testily. "No doubt you would deeply regret any error you might make in the hurry of the moment; but you wouldn't regret it half as much as I should! However, I suppose we've got to trust somebody, as we go through life, and your plan seems, on the whole, as good a one as any."

"Look here, dragon," interrupted the Boy, a little jealous on behalf of his friend, who seemed to be getting all the worst of the bargain: "I don't quite see where *you* come in! There's to be a fight, apparently, and you're to be licked; and what I want to know is, what are *you* going to get out of it?"

"St. George," said the dragon, "just tell him, please—what will happen after I'm vanquished in the deadly combat?"

"Well, according to the rules I suppose I shall lead you in triumph down to the market-place or whatever answers to it," said St. George.

"Precisely," said the dragon. "And then——?"

"And then there'll be shoutings and speeches and things," continued St. George. "And I shall explain that you're converted, and see the error of your ways, and so on."

"Quite so," said the dragon. "And then——?"

"Oh, and then——" said St. George, "why, and then there will be the usual banquet, I suppose."

"Exactly," said the dragon; "and that's where *I* come in. Look here," he continued, addressing the Boy, "I'm bored to death up here, and no one really appreciates me. I'm going into Society, I am, through the kindly aid of our friend here, who's taking such a lot of trouble on my account; and you'll find I've got all the qualities to endear me to people who entertain! So now that's all settled, and if you don't mind—I'm an old-fashioned fellow—don't want to turn you out, but——"

"Remember, you'll have to do your proper share of the fighting, dragon!"

said St. George, as he took the hint and rose to go; "I mean ramping, and breathing fire, and so on!"

"I can *ramp* all right," replied the dragon confidently; "as to breathing fire, it's surprising how easily one gets out of practice; but I'll do the best I can. Good night!"

They had descended the hill and were almost back in the village again, when St. George stopped short. "*Knew* I had forgotten something," he said. "There ought to be a Princess. Terror-stricken and chained to a rock, and all that sort of thing. Boy, can't you arrange a Princess?"

The Boy was in the middle of a tremendous yawn. "I'm tired to death," he wailed, "and I *can't* arrange a Princess, or anything more, at this time of night. And my mother's sitting up, and *do* stop asking me to arrange more things till tomorrow!"

Next morning the people began streaming up to the Downs at quite an early hour, in their Sunday clothes and carrying baskets with bottle-necks sticking out of them, every one intent on securing good places for the combat. This was not exactly a simple matter, for of course it was quite possible that the dragon might win, and in that case even those who had put their money on him felt they could hardly expect him to deal with his backers on a different footing to the rest. Places were chosen, therefore, with circumspection and with a view to a speedy retreat in case of emergency; and the front rank was mostly composed of boys who had escaped from parental control and now sprawled and rolled about on the grass, regardless of the

shrill threats and warnings discharged at them by their anxious mothers behind.

The Boy had secured a good front place, well up towards the cave, and was feeling as anxious as a stage-manager on a first night. Could the dragon be depended upon? He might change his mind and vote the whole performance rot; or else, seeing that the affair had been so hastily planned without even a rehearsal, he might be too nervous to show up. The Boy looked narrowly at the cave, but it showed no sign of life or occupation. Could the dragon have made a moonlight flitting?

The higher portions of the ground were now black with sightseers, and presently a sound of cheering and a waving of handkerchiefs told that something was visible to them which the Boy, far up towards the dragon-end of the line as he was, could not yet see. A minute more and St. George's red plumes topped the hill, as the Saint rode slowly forth on the great level space which stretched up to the grim mouth of the cave. Very gallant and beautiful he looked on his tall war-horse, his golden armour glancing in the sun, his great spear held erect, the little white pennon, crimson-crossed, fluttering at its point. He drew rein and remained motionless. The lines of spectators began to give back a little, nervously; and even the boys in front stopped pulling hair and cuffing each other, and leaned forward expectant.

"Now then, dragon!" muttered the Boy impatiently, fidgeting where he sat. He need not have distressed himself, had he only known. The dramatic possibilities of the thing had tickled the dragon immensely, and he had been up from an early hour, preparing for his first public appearance with as much heartiness as if the years had run backwards, and he had been again a little dragonlet, playing with his sisters on the floor of their mother's cave, at the game of saints-and-dragons, in which the dragon was bound to win.

A low muttering, mingled with snorts, now made itself heard; rising to a bellowing roar that seemed to fill the plain. Then a cloud of smoke obscured the mouth of the cave, and out of the midst of it the dragon himself, shining, sea-blue, magnificent, pranced splendidly forth; and everybody said, "Oo-oo-oo!" as if he had been a mighty rocket! His scales were glittering, his long spiky tail lashed his sides, his claws tore up the turf and sent it flying high over his back, and smoke and fire incessantly jetted from his angry nostrils. "Oh, well done, dragon!" cried the Boy excitedly. "Didn't think he had it in him!" he added to himself.

St. George lowered his spear, bent his head, dug his heels into his horse's sides, and came thundering over the turf. The dragon charged with a roar and a squeal, —a great blue whirling combination of coils and snorts and clashing jaws and spikes and fire.

"Missed!" yelled the crowd. There was a moment's entanglement of golden armour and blue-green coils and spiky tail, and then the great horse, tearing at his bit, carried the Saint, his spear swung high in the air, almost up to the mouth of the cave.

The dragon sat down and barked viciously, while St. George with difficulty pulled his horse round into position.

"End of Round One!" thought the Boy. "How well they managed it! But I hope the Saint won't get excited. I can trust the dragon all right. What a regular play-actor the fellow is!"

St. George had at last prevailed on his horse to stand steady, and was looking round him as he wiped his brow. Catching sight of the Boy, he smiled and nodded, and held up three fingers for an instant.

"It seems to be all planned out," said the Boy to himself. "Round Three is to be the finishing one, evidently. Wish it could have lasted a bit longer. Whatever's that old fool of a dragon up to now?"

The dragon was employing the interval in giving a ramping performance for the benefit of the crowd. Ramping, it should be explained, consists in running round and round in a wide circle, and sending waves and ripples of movement along the whole length of your spine, from your pointed ears right down to the spike at the end of your long tail. When you are covered with blue scales, the effect is particularly pleasing; and the Boy recollected the dragon's recently expressed wish to become a social success.

St. George now gathered up his reins and began to move forward, dropping the point of his spear and settling himself firmly in the saddle.

"Time!" yelled everybody excitedly; and the dragon, leaving off his ramping, sat up on end, and began to leap from one side to the other with huge ungainly bounds, whooping like a Red Indian. This naturally disconcerted the horse, who swerved violently, the Saint only just saving himself by the mane; and as they shot past the dragon delivered a vicious snap at the horse's tail which sent the poor beast careering madly far over the Downs, so that the language of the Saint, who had lost a stirrup, was fortunately inaudible to the general assemblage.

Round Two evoked audible evidence of friendly feelings towards the dragon. The spectators were not slow to appreciate a combatant who could hold his own so well and clearly wanted to show good sport; and many encouraging remarks reached the ears of our friend as he strutted to and fro, his chest thrust out and his tail in the air, hugely enjoying his new popularity.

St. George had dismounted and was tightening his girths, and telling his horse, with quite an Oriental flow of imagery, exactly what he thought of him, and his relations, and his conduct on the present occasion; so the Boy made his way down to the Saint's end of the line, and held his spear for him.

"It's been a jolly fight, St. George!" he said, with a sigh. "Can't you let it last a bit longer?"

"Well, I think I'd better not," replied the Saint. "The fact is, your simple-minded old friend's getting conceited, now they've begun cheering him, and

he'll forget all about the arrangement and take to playing the fool, and there's no telling where he would stop. I'll just finish him off this round."

He swung himself into the saddle and took his spear from the Boy. "Now don't you be afraid," he added kindly. "I've marked my spot exactly, and *he's* sure to give me all the assistance in his power, because he knows it's his only chance of being asked to the banquet!"

St. George now shortened his spear, bringing the butt well up under his arm; and, instead of galloping as before, he trotted smartly towards the dragon, who crouched at his approach, flicking his tail till it cracked in the air like a great cart-whip. The Saint wheeled as he neared his opponent and circled warily round him, keeping his eye on the spare place; while the dragon, adopting similar tactics, paced with caution round the same circle, occasionally feinting with his head. So the two sparred for an opening, while the spectators maintained a breathless silence.

Though the round lasted for some minutes, the end was so swift that all the Boy saw was a lightning movement of the Saint's arm, and then a whirl and a confusion of spines, claws, tail, and flying bits of turf. The dust cleared away, the spectators whooped and ran in cheering, and the Boy made out that the dragon was down, pinned to the earth by the spear, while St. George had dismounted, and stood astride of him.

It all seemed so genuine that the Boy ran in breathlessly, hoping the dear old dragon wasn't really hurt. As he approached, the dragon lifted one large eyelid, winked solemnly, and collapsed again. He was held fast to earth by the neck, but the Saint had hit him in the spare place agreed upon, and it didn't even seem to tickle.

"Bain't you goin' to cut 'is 'ed orf, master?" asked one of the applauding crowd. He had backed the dragon, and naturally felt a trifle sore.

"Well, not *to-day*, I think," replied St. George pleasantly. "You see, that can be done at *any* time. There's no hurry at all. I think we'll all go down to the village first, and have some refreshment, and then I'll give him a good talking-to, and you'll find he'll be a very different dragon!"

At that magic word *refreshment* the whole crowd formed up in procession and silently awaited the signal to start. The time for talking and cheering and betting was past, the hour for action had arrived. St. George, hauling on his spear with both hands, released the dragon, who rose and shook himself and ran his eye over his spikes and scales and things, to see that they were all in order. Then the Saint mounted and led off the procession, the dragon following meekly in the company of the Boy, while the thirsty spectators kept at a respectful interval behind.

There were great doings when they got down to the village again, and had formed up in front of the inn. After refreshment St. George made a speech, in which he informed his audience that he had removed their direful scourge, at a great deal of trouble and inconvenience to himself, and now they weren't to go about grumbling and fancying they'd got grievances, because they hadn't. And they shouldn't be so fond of fights, because next time they might have to do the fighting themselves, which would not be the same thing at all. And there was a certain badger in the inn stables which had got to be released at once, and he'd come and see it done himself. Then he told them that the dragon had been thinking over things, and saw that there were two sides to every question, and he wasn't going to do it any more, and if they were good perhaps he'd stay and settle down there. So they must make friends, and not be prejudiced, and go about fancying they knew everything there was to be known, because they didn't, not by a long way. And he warned them against the sin of romancing, and making up stories and fancying other people would believe them just because they were plausible and highly-coloured. Then he sat down, amidst much repentant cheering, and the dragon nudged the Boy in the ribs and whispered that he couldn't have done it better himself. Then every one went off to get ready for the banquet.

Banquets are always pleasant things, consisting mostly, as they do, of eating and drinking; but the specially nice thing about a banquet is that it comes when something's over, and there's nothing more to worry about, and to-morrow seems a long way off. St. George was happy because there had been a fight and he hadn't had to kill anybody; for he didn't really like killing, though he generally had to do it. The dragon was happy because there had been a fight, and far from being hurt in it so he had won popularity and a sure footing in Society. The Boy was happy because there had been a fight, and in spite of it all his two friends were on the best of terms. And all the others were happy because there had been a fight, and—well, they didn't require any other reasons for their happiness. The dragon exerted himself to say the right thing to everybody, and proved the life and soul of the evening; while the Saint and the Boy, as they looked on, felt that they were only assisting at a feast of which the honour and the glory were entirely the dragon's. But they didn't mind that, being good fellows, and the dragon was not in the least proud or forgetful. On the contrary, every ten minutes or so he leant over towards the Boy and said impressively: "Look here! you *will* see me home afterwards, won't you?" And the Boy always nodded, though he had promised his mother not to be out late.

At last the banquet was over, the guests had dropped away with many good nights and congratulations and invitations, and the dragon, who had seen the last of them off the premises, emerged into the street followed by the Boy, wiped his brow, sighed, sat down in the road and gazed at the stars. "Jolly night it's been!" he murmured. "Jolly stars! Jolly litle place this! Think I shall just stop here. Don't feel like climbing up any beastly hill. Boy's promised to see me home. Boy had better do it then! No responsibility on my part. Responsibility all Boy's!" And his chin sank on his broad chest and he slumbered peacefully.

"Oh, *get* up, dragon," cried the Boy piteously. "You *know* my mother's sitting up, and I'm so tired, and you made me promise to see you home, and I never knew what it meant or I wouldn't have done it!" And the Boy sat down in the

road by the side of the sleeping dragon, and cried.

The door behind them opened, a stream of light illumined the road, and St. George, who had come out for a stroll in the cool night-air, caught sight of the two figures sitting there—the great motionless dragon and the tearful little Boy.

"What's the matter, Boy?" he inquired kindly, stepping to his side.

"Oh, it's this great lumbering *pig* of a dragon!" sobbed the Boy. "First he makes me promise to see him home, and then he says I'd better do it, and goes to sleep! Might as well try to see a *haystack* home! And I'm so tired, and mother's——" Here he broke down again.

"Now don't take on," said St. George. "I'll stand by you, and we'll *both* see him home. Wake up, dragon!" he said sharply, shaking the beast by the elbow.

The dragon looked up sleepily. "What a night, George!" he murmured; "what a——"

"Now look here, dragon," said the Saint firmly. "Here's this little fellow waiting to see you home, and you *know* he ought to have been in bed these two hours, and what his mother'll say *I* don't know, and anybody but a selfish pig would have *made* him go to bed long ago——"

"And he *shall* go to bed!" cried the dragon, starting up. "Poor little chap, only fancy his being up at this hour! It's a shame, that's what it is, and I don't think, St. George, you've been very considerate—but come along at once, and don't let us have any more arguing or shilly-shallying. You give me hold of your hand, Boy—thank you, George, an arm up the hill is just what I wanted!"

So they set off up the hill arm-in-arm, the Saint, the dragon, and the Boy. The lights in the little village began to go out; but there were stars, and a late moon, as they climbed to the Downs together.

And, as they turned the last corner and disappeared from view, snatches of an old song were borne back on the night breeze. I can't be certain which of them was singing, but I *think* it was the dragon!

35

It is hard to believe that
the worldly and cynical poet and playwright, Oscar Wilde,
was the same man who wrote some of the simplest and most
beautiful of modern fairy tales.
"The Selfish Giant" is one of these.
It is a touching tale of an overgrown and overbearing creature
who built a high wall to keep children out of his garden and,
as a consequence, shut out the sunshine and all happiness.
How the song of a small bird made him break down the wall,
and how a boy he comes to love suddenly disappears—
this is the secret of a story that
turns into much more than a story.

The Selfish Giant

BY OSCAR WILDE
Illustrated by DENVER GILLEN

EVERY AFTERNOON, as they were coming from school, the children used to go and play in the Giant's garden.

It was a large lovely garden, with soft green grass. Here and there over the grass stood beautiful flowers like stars, and there were twelve peach-trees that in the springtime broke out into delicate blossoms of pink and pearl, and in the autumn bore rich fruit. The birds sat on the trees and sang so sweetly that the children used to stop their games in order to listen to them. "How happy we are here!" they cried to each other.

One day the Giant came back. He had been to visit his friend the Cornish ogre, and had stayed with him for seven years. After the seven years were over he had said all that he had to say, for his conversation was limited, and he determined to return to his own castle. When he arrived he saw the children playing in the garden.

"What are you doing there?" he cried in a very gruff voice, and the children ran away.

"My own garden is my own garden," said the Giant; "any one can understand that, and I will allow nobody to play in it but myself." So he built a high wall all around it, and put up a notice-board.

TRESPASSERS
WILL BE
PROSECUTED

He was a very selfish Giant.

The poor children had now nowhere to play. They tried to play on the road, but the road was very dusty and full of hard stones, and they did not like it. They used to wander round the high wall when their lessons were over, and talk about the beautiful garden inside. "How happy we were there," they said to each other.

Then the Spring came, and all over the country there were little blossoms and little birds. Only in the garden of the selfish Giant it was still winter. The birds did not care to sing in it as there were no children, and the trees forgot to blossom. Once a beautiful flower put its head out from the grass, but when it saw the notice-board it was so sorry for the children that it slipped back into the ground again, and went off to sleep. The only people who were pleased were the Snow and the Frost. "Spring has forgotten this garden," they cried, "so we will live here all the year round." The Snow covered up the grass with her great white cloak, and the Frost painted all the trees silver. Then they invited the North Wind to stay with them, and he came. He was wrapped in furs, and he roared all day about the garden, and blew the chimney-pots down. "This is a delightful spot," he said, "we must ask the Hail on a visit." So the Hail came. Every day for three hours he rattled on the roof of the castle till he broke most of the slates, and then he ran round and round the garden as fast as he could go.

He was dressed in grey, and his breath was like ice.

"I cannot understand why the Spring is so late in coming," said the Selfish Giant, as he sat at the window and looked out at his cold white garden; "I hope there will be a change in the weather."

But the Spring never came, nor the Summer. The Autumn gave golden fruit to every garden, but to the Giant's garden she gave none. "He is too selfish," she said. So it was always Winter there, and the North Wind, and the Hail, and the Frost, and the Snow danced about through the trees.

One morning the Giant was lying awake in bed when he heard some lovely music. It sounded so sweet to his ears that he thought it must be the King's musicians passing by. It was really only a little linnet singing outside his window, but it was so long since he had heard a bird sing in his garden that it seemed to him to be the most beautiful music in the world. Then the Hail stopped dancing over his head, and the North Wind ceased roaring, and a delicious perfume came to him through the open casement. "I believe the Spring has come at last," said the Giant; and he jumped out of bed and looked out.

What did he see?

He saw a most wonderful sight. Through a little hole in the wall the children had crept in, and they were sitting in the branches of the trees. In every tree that he could see there was a little child. And the trees were so glad to have the children back again that they had covered themselves with blossoms, and were waving their arms gently above the children's heads. The birds were flying about and twittering with delight, and the flowers were looking up through the green grass and laughing. It was a lovely scene; only in one corner it was still winter. It was the farthest corner of the garden, and in it was standing a little boy. He was so small that he could not reach up to the branches of the tree, and he was wandering all around it, crying bitterly. The poor tree was still quite covered with frost and snow, and

the North Wind was blowing and roaring about it. "Climb up! little boy," said the tree, and it bent its branches down as low as it could; but the boy was too tiny.

And the Giant's heart melted as he looked out. "How selfish I have been!" he said; "now I know why the Spring would not come here. I will put that poor little boy on the top of the tree, and then I will knock down the wall, and my garden shall be the children's playground for ever and ever."

He was really very sorry for what he had done.

So he crept downstairs and opened the front door quite softly, and went out into the garden. But when the children saw him they were so frightened that they all ran away, and the garden became winter again. Only the little boy did not run, for his eyes were so full of tears that he did not see the Giant coming. And the Giant stole up behind him and took him gently in his hand, and

39

put him up into the tree. And the tree broke at once into blossom, and the birds came and sang on it, and the little boy stretched out his two arms and flung them round the Giant's neck, and kissed him. And the other children, when they saw that the Giant was not wicked any longer, came running back, and with them came the Spring. "It is your garden now, little children," said the Giant, and he took a great axe and knocked down the wall. And when the people were going to market at twelve o'clock they found the Giant playing with the children in the most beautiful garden they had ever seen. All day long they played, and in the evening they came to the Giant to bid him good-bye.

"But where is your little companion?" he said, "the boy I put into the tree?" The Giant loved him the best because he had kissed him.

"We don't know," answered the children; "he has gone away."

"You must tell him to be sure and come here tomorrow," said the Giant. But the children said that they did not know where he lived, and had never seen him before; and the Giant felt very sad.

Every afternoon, when school was over, the children came and played with the Giant. But the little boy whom the Giant loved was never seen again. The Giant was very kind to all the children, yet he longed for his first little friend, and often spoke of him. "How I would like to see him!" he used to say.

Years went over, and the Giant grew very old and feeble. He could not play about any more, so he sat in a huge armchair, and watched the children at their games, and admired his garden. "I have many beautiful flowers," he said; "but the children are the most beautiful flowers of all."

One winter morning he looked out of his window as he was dressing. He did not hate the Winter now, for he knew that is was merely the Spring asleep, and that the flowers were resting.

Suddenly he rubbed his eyes in wonder, and looked and looked. It certainly was a marvellous sight. In the farthest corner of the garden was a tree quite covered with lovely white blossoms. Its branches were all golden, and silver fruit hung down from them, and underneath it stood the little boy he had loved.

Downstairs ran the Giant in great joy, and out into the garden. He hastened across the grass, and came near to the child. And when he came quite close his face grew red with anger, and he said, "Who hath dared to wound thee?" For on the palms of the child's hands were the prints of two nails, and the prints of two nails were on the little feet.

"Who hath dared to wound thee?" cried the Giant; "tell me, that I may take my sword and slay him."

"Nay!" answered the child; "but these are the wounds of Love."

"Who art thou?" said the Giant, and a strange awe fell on him, and he knelt before the little child.

And the child smiled on the Giant, and said to him, "You let me play once in your garden; today you shall come with me to my garden, which is Paradise."

And when the children ran in that afternoon, they found the Giant lying dead under the tree, all covered with white blossoms.

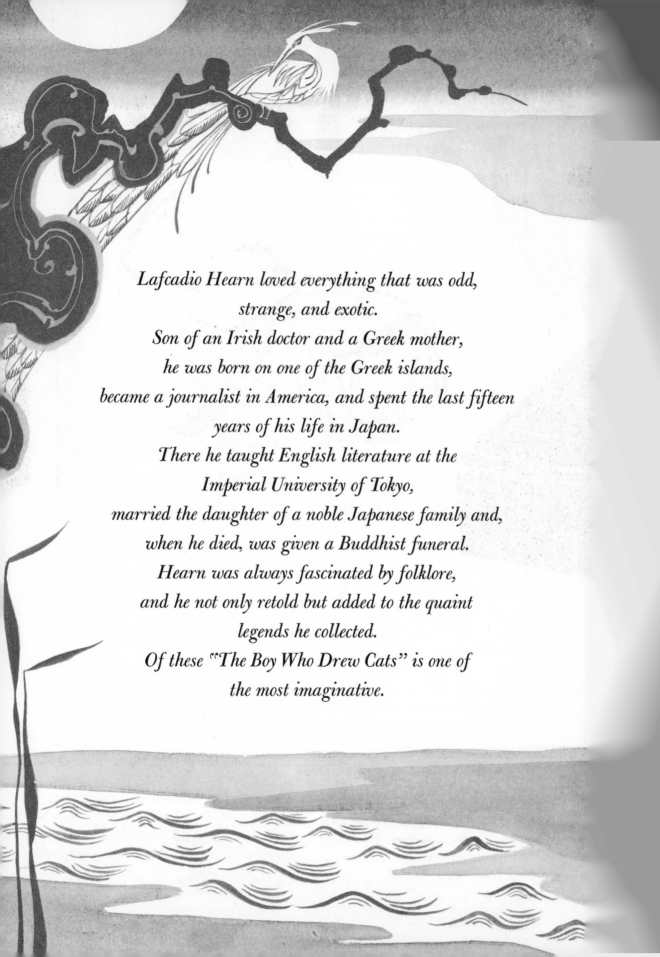

Lafcadio Hearn loved everything that was odd,
strange, and exotic.
Son of an Irish doctor and a Greek mother,
he was born on one of the Greek islands,
became a journalist in America, and spent the last fifteen
years of his life in Japan.
There he taught English literature at the
Imperial University of Tokyo,
married the daughter of a noble Japanese family and,
when he died, was given a Buddhist funeral.
Hearn was always fascinated by folklore,
and he not only retold but added to the quaint
legends he collected.
Of these "The Boy Who Drew Cats" is one of
the most imaginative.

The Boy Who Drew Cats

BY LAFCADIO HEARN
Illustrated by GORDON LAITE

A LONG, LONG TIME AGO, in a small country village in Japan, there lived a poor farmer and his wife, who were very good people. They had a number of children, and found it very hard to feed them all. The elder son was strong enough when only fourteen years old to help his father; and the little girls learned to help their mother almost as soon as they could walk.

But the youngest child, a little boy, did not seem to be fit for hard work. He was very clever—cleverer than all his brothers and sisters, but he was quite weak and small, and people said he could never grow very big. So his parents thought it would be better for him to become a priest than to become a farmer. They took him with them to the village temple one day, and asked the good old

42

priest who lived there, if he would have their little boy for his attendant, and teach him all that a priest ought to know.

The old man spoke kindly to the lad, and asked him some hard questions. So clever were the answers that the priest agreed to take the little fellow into the temple as an acolyte, and to educate him for the priesthood.

The boy learned quickly what the old priest taught him, and was very obedient in most things. But he had one fault. He liked to draw cats during study hours, and to draw cats even where cats ought not to have been drawn at all.

Whenever he found himself alone, he drew cats. He drew them on the margins of the priest's books, and on all the screens of the temple, and on the walls, and on the pillars. Several times the priest told him this was not right; but he did not stop drawing cats. He drew them because he could not really help it. He had what is called "the genius of an *artist*," and just for that reason he was not quite fit to be an acolyte; a good acolyte should study books.

One day after he had drawn some very clever pictures of cats upon a paper screen, the old priest said to him severely: "My boy, you must go away from this temple at once. You will never make a good priest, but perhaps you will become a great artist. Now let me give you a last piece of advice, and be sure you never forget it. *Avoid large places at night; keep to small!*"

The boy did not know what the priest meant my saying, "*Avoid large places; keep to small.*" He thought and thought, while he was tying up his little bundle of clothes to go away. But he could not understand those words, and he was afraid to speak to the priest any more, except to say good-bye.

He left the temple very sorrowfully, and began to wonder what he should do. If he went straight home he felt sure his father would punish him for having been disobedient to the priest: so he was afraid to go home. All at once he remembered that at the next village, twelve miles away, there was a very big temple. He had heard there were several priests at that temple, and he made up his mind to go to them and ask them to take him for their acolyte.

Now that big temple was closed up but the boy did not know this fact. The reason it had been closed up was that a goblin had frightened the priests away, and had taken possession of the place. Some brave warriors had afterward gone to the temple at night to kill the goblin; but they had never been seen alive again. Nobody had ever told these things to the boy—so he walked all the way to the village hoping to be kindly treated by the priests.

When he got to the village it was already dark, and all the people were in bed; but he saw the big temple on a hill at the other end of the principal street, and he saw there was a light in the temple. People who tell the story say the goblin used to make that light in order to tempt lonely travelers to ask for shelter. The boy went at once to the temple and knocked. There was no sound inside. He knocked and knocked again; but still nobody came. At last he pushed gently at the door, and was glad to find that it has not been fastened. So he went in, and saw a lamp burning—but no priest.

He thought some priest would be sure to come very soon, and he sat down and waited. Then he noticed that everything in the temple was gray with dust, and thickly spun over with cobwebs. So he thought to himself that the priests would certainly like to have an acolyte, to keep the place clean. He wondered why they had allowed everything to get so dusty. What most pleased him, however, were some big white screens, good to paint cats upon. Though he was tired, he looked at once for a writing-box, and found one, and ground some ink, and began to paint cats.

He painted a great many cats upon the screens; and then he began to feel very, very sleepy. He was just on the point of lying down to sleep beside one of the screens, when he suddenly remembered the words, *"Avoid large places; keep to small!"*

The temple was very large; he was all alone; and as he thought of these words

—though he could not quite understand them—he began to feel for the first time a little afraid; and he resolved to look for a *small place* in which to sleep. He found a little cabinet with a sliding door, and went into it, and shut himself up. Then he lay down and fell fast asleep.

Very late in the night he was awakened by a most terrible noise—a noise of fighting and screaming. It was so dreadful that he was afraid even to look through a chink of the little cabinet: he lay very still, holding his breath for fright. The light that had been in the temple went out; but the awful sounds continued, and became more awful, and all the temple shook. After a long time silence came; but the boy was still afraid to move. He did not move until the light of the morning sun shone into the cabinet through the chinks of the little door.

Then he got out of his hiding-place very cautiously, and looked about. The first thing he saw was that all the floor of the temple was covered with blood. And then he saw, lying dead, in the middle of it, an enormous, monstrous rat —a goblin rat— bigger than a cow!

But who or what could have killed it? There was no man or other creature to be seen. Suddenly the boy observed that the mouths of all the cats he had drawn the night before were red and wet with blood. Then he knew that the goblin had been killed by the cats which he had drawn. And then also, for the first time, he understood why the wise old priest had said to him, *"Avoid large places at night; keep to small."*

Afterward that boy became a very famous artist. Some of the cats which he drew are still shown to travelers in Japan.

44

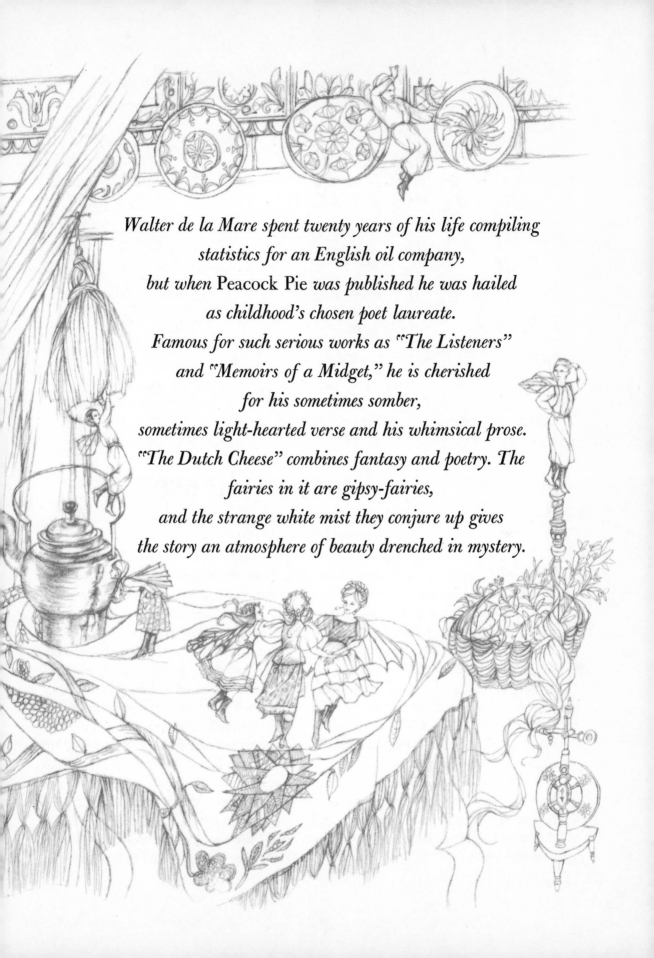

Walter de la Mare spent twenty years of his life compiling
statistics for an English oil company,
but when Peacock Pie was published he was hailed
as childhood's chosen poet laureate.
Famous for such serious works as "The Listeners"
and "Memoirs of a Midget," he is cherished
for his sometimes somber,
sometimes light-hearted verse and his whimsical prose.
"The Dutch Cheese" combines fantasy and poetry. The
fairies in it are gipsy-fairies,
and the strange white mist they conjure up gives
the story an atmosphere of beauty drenched in mystery.

The Dutch Cheese

BY WALTER DE LA MARE
Illustrated by JEAN WINSLOW

ONCE—once upon a time there lived, with his sister Griselda, in a little cottage near the Great Forest, a young farmer whose name was John. Brother and sister, they lived alone except for their sheepdog, Sly, their flock of sheep, the numberless birds of the forest, and the fairies. John loved his sister beyond telling; he loved Sly; and he delighted to listen to the birds singing at twilight round the darkening margin of the forest. But he feared and hated the fairies. And, having a very stubborn heart, the more he feared, the more he hated them; and the more he hated them, the more they pestered him.

Now these were a tribe of fairies, sly, small, gay-hearted and mischievous, and not of the race of fairies noble, silent, beautiful and remote from man. They were a sort of gipsy-fairies, very nimble and of aery and prankish company, and partly for mischief and partly for love of her they were always trying to charm John's dear sister Griselda away, with their music and fruits and trickery. He more than half believed it was they who years ago had decoyed into the forest not only his poor old father, who had gone out faggot-cutting in his sheepskin hat with his ass; but his mother too, who soon after, had gone out to look for him.

But fairies, even of this small tribe, hate no man. They mocked him and mischiefed him; they spilt his milk, rode astraddle on his rams, garlanded his old ewes with sow-thistle and briony, sprinkled water on his kindling wood, loosed his bucket in the well, and hid his great leather shoes. But all this they did not for hate—for they came and went like evening moths about Griselda—but because in his fear and fury he shut up his sister from them, and because he was sullen and stupid. Yet he did nothing but fret himself. He set traps for them, and caught starlings; he fired his blunderbuss at them under the moon, and scared his sheep; he set dishes of sour milk in their way, and sticky leaves and brambles where their rings were green in the meadows; but all to no purpose. When at dusk, too, he heard their faint, elfin music, he would sit in the door blowing into his father's great bassoon till the black forest re-echoed with its sad, solemn, wooden voice. But that was of no help either. At last he grew so surly that he made Griselda utterly miserable. Her cheeks lost their scarlet and her eyes their sparkling. Then the fairies began to plague John in earnest—lest their lovely, loved child of man, Griselda, should die.

Now one summer's evening—and most nights are cold in the Great Forest—John, having put away his mournful bassoon and bolted the door, was squatting, moody and gloomy, with Griselda, on his hearth beside the fire. And he leaned back his great hairy head and stared straight up the chimney to where high in the heavens glittered a host of stars. And suddenly, while he lolled there on his stool moodily watching them, there appeared against the dark sky a mischievous elfish head secretly peeping down at him; and busy fingers began sprinkling dew on his wide upturned face. He heard the laughter too of the fairies miching and gambolling on his thatch, and in his rage he started up, seized a round Dutch cheese that lay on a platter, and with all his force threw it clean and straight up the sooty chimney at the faces of mockery clustered above. And after that, though Griselda sighed at her spinning wheel, he heard no more. Even the cricket that had been whistling all through the evening fell silent, and John supped on his black bread and onions alone.

Next day Griselda woke at dawn and put her head out of the little window beneath the thatch, and the day was white with mist.

" 'Twill be another hot day," she said to herself, combing her beautiful hair.

But when John went down, so white and dense with mist were the fields, that even the green borders of the forest were invisible, and the whiteness went to the sky. Swathing and wreathing itself, opal and white as milk, all the morning the mist grew thicker and thicker about the little house. When John went out about nine o'clock to peer about him, nothing was to be seen at all. He could hear his sheep bleating, the kettle singing, Griselda sweeping, but straight up above him hung only, like a small round fruit, a little cheese-red beamless sun—straight up above him, though the hands of the clock were not yet come to ten. He clenched his fists and stamped in sheer rage. But no-one answered him, no voice mocked him but his own. For when these idle, mischievous fairies have played a trick on an enemy they soon weary of it.

All day long that little sullen lantern burned above the mist, sometimes red, so that the white mist was dyed to amber, and sometimes milky pale. The trees dripped water from every leaf. Every flower asleep in the garden was neckleted with beads; and nothing but a drenched old forest crow visited the lonely cottage that afternoon to cry: "Kah, Kah, Kah!" and fly away.

But Griselda knew her brother's mood too well to speak of it, or to complain. And she sang on gaily in the house, though she was more sorrowful than ever.

Next day John went out to tend his flocks. And wherever he went the red sun seemed to follow. When at last he found his sheep they were drenched with the clinging mist and were huddled together in dismay. And when they saw him it seemed that they cried out with one unanimous bleating voice:

"O ma-a-a-ster!"

And he stood counting them. And a little apart from the rest stood his old ram Soll, with a face as black as soot; and there, perched on his back, impish and sharp and scarlet, rode and tossed and sang just such another fairy as had mocked John from the chimney-top. A fire seemed to break out in his body, and, picking up a handful of stones, he rushed at Soll through the flock. They scattered, bleating, out into the mist. And the fairy, all-acockahoop on the old ram's back, took its small ears between finger and thumb, and as fast as John ran, so fast jogged Soll, till all the young

farmer's stones were thrown, and he found himself alone in a quagmire so sticky and befogged that it took him till afternoon to grope his way out. And only Griselda's singing over her broth-pot guided him at last home.

Next day he sought his sheep far and wide, but not one could he find. To and fro he wandered, shouting and calling and whistling to Sly, till heartsick and thirsty, they were both wearied out. Yet bleatings seemed to fill the air, and a faint, beautiful bell tolled on out of the mist; and John knew the fairies had hidden his sheep, and he hated them more than ever.

After that he went no more into the fields, brightly green beneath the enchanted mist. He sat and sulked, staring out of the door at the dim forests far away, glimmering faintly red beneath the small red sun. Griselda could not sing anymore, she was too tired and hungry. And just before twilight she went out and gathered the last few pods of peas from the garden for their supper.

And while she was shelling them, John, within doors in the cottage, heard again the tiny timbrels and the distant horns, and the odd, clear, grasshopper voices calling and calling her, and he knew in his heart that, unless he relented and made friends with the fairies, Griselda would surely one day run away to them and leave him forlorn. He scratched his great head, and gnawed his broad thumb. They had taken his father, they had taken his mother, they might take his sister—but he *wouldn't* give in.

So he shouted, and Griselda in fear and trembling came in out of the garden with her basket and basin and sat down in the gloaming to finish shelling her peas.

And as the shadows thickened and the stars began to shine, the malevolent singing came nearer, and presently there was a groping and stirring in the thatch, a tapping at the window, and John knew the fairies had come—not alone, not one or two or three, but in their company and bands—to plague him, and to entice away Griselda. He shut his mouth and stopped up his ears with his fingers, but when, with great staring eyes, he saw them capering like bubbles in a glass, like flames along straw, on his very doorstep, he could contain himself no longer. He caught up Griselda's bowl and flung it—peas, water and all—full in the snickering faces of the Little Folk! There came a shrill, faint twitter of laughter, a scampering of feet, and then all again was utterly still.

Griselda tried in vain to keep back her tears. She put her arms round John's neck and hid her face in his sleeve.

"Let me go!" she said, "let me go, John, just a day and a night, and I'll come back to you. They are angry with us. But they love me; and if I sit on the hillside under the boughs of the trees beside the pool and listen to their music just a little while, they will make the sun shine again and drive back the flocks, and we shall be as happy as ever. Look at poor Sly, John dear, he is hungrier even than I am." John heard only the mocking laughter and the tap-tapping and the rustling and crying of the fairies, and he wouldn't let his sister go.

And it began to be marvellously dark

and still in the cottage. No stars moved across the casement, no waterdrops glittered in the candleshine. John could hear only one low, faint, unceasing stir and rustling all round him. So utterly dark and still it was that even Sly woke from his hungry dreams and gazed up into his mistress's face and whined.

They went to bed; but still, all night long, while John lay tossing on his mattress, the rustling never ceased. The old kitchen clock ticked on and on, but there came no hint of dawn. All was pitch-black and now all was utterly silent. There wasn't a whisper, not a creak, not a sigh of air, not a footfall of mouse, not a flutter of moth, not a settling of dust to be heard at all. Only desolate silence. And John at last could endure his fears and suspicions no longer. He got out of bed and stared from his square casement. He could see nothing. He tried to thrust it open; it would not move. He

went downstairs and unbarred the door and looked out. He saw, as it were, a deep, clear, green shade, from behind which the songs of the birds rose faint as in a dream.

And then he sighed like a grampus and sat down, and knew that the fairies had beaten him. Like Jack's beanstalk, in one night had grown up a dense wall of peas. He pushed and pulled and hacked with his axe, and kicked with his shoes, and buffeted with his blunderbuss. But it was all in vain. He sat down once more in his chair beside the hearth and covered his face with his hands. And at last Griselda, too, awoke, and came down with her candle. And she comforted her brother, and told him if he would do what she bade she would soon make all right again. And he promised her.

So with a scarf she bound tight his hands behind him; and with a rope she bound his feet together, so that he could neither run nor throw stones, peas or cheeses. She bound his eyes and ears and mouth with a napkin, so that he could neither see, hear, smell, nor cry out. And, that done, she pushed and pulled him like a great bundle, and at last rolled him out of sight into the chimney-corner against the wall. Then she took a small sharp pair of needlework scissors that her godmother had given her, and snipped and snipped, till at last there came a little hole in the thick green hedge of peas. And putting her mouth there she called softly through the little hole. And the fairies drew near the door-step and nodded and nodded and listened.

And then and there Griselda made a

bargain with them for the forgiveness of John—a lock of her golden hair; seven dishes of ewes' milk; three and thirty bunches of currants, red, white and black; a bag of thistledown; three handkerchiefs full of lambs' wool; nine jars of honey; a peppercorn of spice. All these (except the hair) John was to bring himself to their secret places as soon as he was able. Above all, the bargain between them was that Griselda would sit one full hour each evening of summer on the hillside in the shadow and greenness that slope down from the Great Forest towards the valley, where the fairies' mounds are, and where their tiny brindled cattle graze.

Her brother lay blind and deaf and dumb as a log of wood. She promised everything.

And then, instead of a rustling and a creeping, there came a rending and a crashing. Instead of green shade, light of amber; then white. And as the thick hedge withered and shrank, and the merry and furious dancing sun scorched and scorched and scorched, there came, above the singing of the birds, the bleatings of sheep—and behold, sooty Soll and hungry Sly met square upon the doorstep; and all John's sheep shone white as hoar-frost on his pastures; and every lamb was garlanded with pimpernel and eyebright; and the old fat ewes stood still, with saddles of moss, and their laughing riders sat and saw Griselda standing in the doorway in her beautiful yellow hair.

As for John, tied up like a sack in the chimney-corner, down came his cheese again crash upon his head, and, not being able to say anything, he said nothing.

The next three stories revolve around
the cleverness or character not of man but of the creatures
with which he shares the world. In each story there is a contest:
Who will win the Princess?
Will the wolf destroy the faithful dog?
Will the man tell his wife the secret that will cost him his life?
The answers lie in the instinctive wisdom of
animal, insect, and bird.

The Leaping Match

BY HANS CHRISTIAN ANDERSEN
Illustrated by GORDON LAITE

THE FLEA, the grasshopper, and the frog once wished to try which of them could jump highest; so they invited the whole world, and anybody else who liked, to come and see the grand sight. They were all three first-rate jumpers, as every one saw when they met together in the room.

"I will give my daughter to him who shall jump highest," said the King. "It would be too bad for you to have to jump for nothing." The flea came first. He had very polite manners, and bowed to the company on every side, for he was of noble blood; besides, he was accustomed to man, and that always makes a great difference.

Next came the grasshopper. He was certainly of a heavier build, but all the same he had a good figure and wore a green uniform, which belonged to him by right of birth. Besides, he was said to have sprung from a very high Egyptian family, and to be greatly thought of in that country. He had been taken out of the field where he learned to jump and put into a card house three stories high.

53

This house was built on purpose for him, and all of court-cards, the faces being turned inwards. As for the doors and windows, they were all cut out of the Queen of Hearts.

"And I can sing so well," said he, "that sixteen parlour-bred crickets, who have chirped and chirped and chirped ever since they were born, and yet could never get anybody to build them a card house, after hearing me, have fretted themselves ten times thinner than they were before, from jealousy."

Both the flea and the grasshopper knew how to make the most of themselves, and each thought himself quite a match for a Princess.

The frog said not a word; however, it might be that he thought the more. The house-dog, after sniffing about him carefully, stated that the frog must be of a good family. And the King's old and trusted councillor, who had received three medals for holding his tongue, declared that the frog must be gifted with the spirit of prophecy, and that one could tell from his back whether there was to be a severe or a mild winter, which was more than could be read from the back of the man who wrote the Almanac.

"I will say nothing for the present," said the old King, "but I will observe everything, and form my own opinion. Let them show us what they can do."

And now the match began.

The flea jumped so high that no one could see what had become of him, and so they insisted that he had not jumped at all, "which was disgraceful, after he had made such a fuss!"

The grasshopper only jumped half as high, but he jumped right into the King's face, and the King declared he was quite disgusted by his rudeness.

The frog stood still as if lost in thought; and people began to think he did not mean to jump at all.

"I'm afraid he is ill!" said the dog; and he went sniffing at him again to see if he could find out what was wrong, when, lo! all at once the frog made a little jump into the lap of the Princess, who was sitting on a low gold stool close by. Then the King gave his judgment.

"There is nothing higher than my daughter," said he; "therefore it is plain that he who jumps up to her jumps highest; but only a person of good understanding would ever have thought of that, so the frog has shown us that he has understanding."

And thus the frog won the Princess.

"I jumped highest, for all that!" said the flea. "But it's all the same to me. Let her have the stiff-legged, slimy creature, if she likes! I jumped highest; but dullness and heaviness win the day with people in this stupid world."

And so the flea went away and fought in foreign wars, where, it is said, he was killed.

As for the grasshopper, he sat on a green bank, and thought on the world and its strange goings on, and at length he repeated the flea's last words. "Yes," he said, "dullness and heaviness win the day! dullness and heaviness win the day!" And then he again began singing his own melancholy song, and it is from him that we have learnt this story, and yet, my friend, though you read it here in a printed book, it may not be perfectly true.

54

Old Sultan

BY JAKOB AND WILHELM GRIMM
Illustrated by GORDON LAITE

A SHEPHERD had a faithful dog, called Sultan, who was grown very old, and had lost all his teeth. And one day when the shepherd and his wife were standing together before the house the shepherd said, "I will shoot old Sultan tomorrow morning, for he is of no use now." But his wife said, "Pray let the poor faithful creature live; he has served us well a great many years, and we ought to give him a livelihood for the rest of his days." "But what can we do with him?" said the shepherd; "he has not a tooth in his head, and the thieves don't care for him at all. To be sure he has served us, but then he did it

to earn his livelihood; tomorrow shall be his last day, depend upon it."

Poor Sultan, who was lying close by them, heard all that the shepherd and his wife said to one another, and was very much frightened to think tomorrow would be his last day; so in the evening he went to his good friend the wolf, who lived in the wood, and told him all his sorrows, and how his master meant to kill him in the morning.

"Make yourself easy," said the wolf, "I will give you some good advice. Your master, you know, goes out every morning very early with his wife into the field; and they take their little child with them, and lay it down behind the hedge in the shade while they are at work. Now do you lie down close by the child, and pretend to be watching it, and I will come out of the wood and run away with it; you must run after me as fast as you can, and I will let it drop; then you may carry it back, and they will think you have saved their child, and will be so thankful to you that they will take care of you as long as you live." The dog liked this plan very well; and accordingly so it was managed. The wolf ran with the child a little way; the shepherd and his wife screamed out; but Sultan soon overtook him, and carried the poor little thing back to his master and mistress. Then the shepherd patted him on the head, and said, "Old Sultan has saved our child from the wolf, and therefore he shall live and be well taken care of, and have plenty to eat. Wife, go home, and give him a good dinner, and let him have my old cushion to sleep on as long as he lives." So from this time forward Sultan had all that he could wish for.

Soon afterwards the wolf came and wished him joy, and said, "Now, my good fellow, you must tell no tales, but turn your head the other way when I want to taste one of the old shepherd's fine sheep." "No," said Sultan; "I will be true to my master." However, the wolf thought he was joking, and came one night to get a dainty morsel. But Sultan had told his master what the wolf meant to do; so he laid in wait for him behind the barn-door, and when the wolf was busy looking out for a good sheep, he had a stout cudgel laid about his back, that combed his locks for him finely.

Then the wolf was very angry, and called Sultan "an old rogue," and swore he would have his revenge. So the next morning the wolf sent the boar to challenge Sultan to come into the wood to fight the matter out. Now Sultan had nobody he could ask to be his second but the shepherd's old three-legged cat; so he took her with him, and as the poor thing limped along with some trouble, she stuck up her tail straight in the air.

The wolf and the wild boar were first on the ground; and when they espied their enemies coming, and saw the cat's long tail standing straight in the air, they thought she was carrying a sword for Sultan to fight with; and every time she limped, they thought she was picking up a stone to throw at them; so they said they should not like this way of fighting, and the boar lay down behind a bush, and the wolf jumped up into a tree.

Sultan and the cat soon came up, and looked about, and wondered that no one was there. The boar, however, had not quite hidden himself, for his ears stuck out of the bush; and when he shook one of them a little, the cat, seeing something move, and thinking it was a mouse, sprang upon it, and bit and scratched it, so that the boar jumped up and grunted, and ran away, roaring out, "Look up in the tree; there sits the one who is to blame!"

So they looked up, and espied the wolf sitting amongst the branches; and they called him a cowardly rascal, and would not suffer him to come down till he was heartily ashamed of himself, and had promised to be good friends again with old Sultan.

The Language of Beasts

EDITED BY ANDREW LANG
Illustrated by GORDON LAITE

ONCE UPON a time a man had a shepherd who served him many years faithfully and honestly. One day, whilst herding his flock, this shepherd heard a hissing sound, coming out of the forest near by, which he could not account for. So he went into the wood in the direction of the noise to try to discover the cause. When he approached the place he found that the dry grass and leaves were on fire, and on a tree, surrounded by flames, a snake was coiled, hissing with terror.

The shepherd stood wondering how the poor snake could escape, for the wind was blowing the flames that way, and soon that tree would be burning like the rest. Suddenly the snake cried: "O shepherd! for the love of heaven save me from this fire!"

Then the shepherd stretched his staff out over the flames and the snake wound itself round the staff and up to his hand, and from his hand it crept up his arm, and twined itself about his neck. The shepherd trembled with fright, expecting every instant to be stung to death, and said: "What an unlucky man I am! Did I rescue you only to be destroyed myself?" But the snake answered: "Have no fear; only carry me home to my father who is the King of the Snakes." The shepherd, however, was much too frightened to listen, and said that he could not go away and leave his flock alone; but the snake said: "You need not be afraid to leave your flock, no evil shall befall them; but make all the haste you can."

58

So he set off through the wood carrying the snake, and after a time he came to a great gateway, made entirely of snakes intertwined one with another. The shepherd stood still with surprise, but the snake round his neck whistled, and immediately all the arch unwound itself.

"When we are come to my father's house," said his own snake to him, "he will reward you with anything you like to ask—silver, gold, jewels, or whatever on this earth is most precious. But take none of all these things; ask rather to understand the language of beasts. He will refuse it to you a long time, but in the end he will grant it to you."

Soon after that they arrived at the house of the King of the Snakes, who burst into tears of joy at the sight of his daughter, as he had given her up for dead. "Where have you been all this time?" he asked, directly he could speak, and she told him that she had been caught in a forest fire, and had been rescued from the flames by the shepherd. The King of the Snakes, then turning to the shepherd, said to him: "What reward will you choose for saving my child?"

"Make me to know the language of beasts," answered the shepherd, "that is all I desire."

The king replied: "Such knowledge would be of no benefit to you, for if I granted it to you and you told any one of it, you would immediately die; ask me rather for whatever else you would most like to possess, and it shall be yours."

But the shepherd answered him: "Sir, if you wish to reward me for saving your daughter, grant me, I pray you, to know the language of beasts. I desire nothing else"; and he turned as if to depart.

Then the king called him back, saying: "If nothing else will satisfy you, open your mouth." The man obeyed, and the king spat into it, and said: "Now spit into my mouth." The shepherd did as he was told; then the King of the Snakes spat again into the shepherd's mouth. When they had spat into each other's mouths three times, the king said: "Now you know the language of beasts, go in peace; but, if you value your life, beware lest you tell anyone of it, else you will immediately die."

So the shepherd set out for home, and on his way through the wood he heard and understood all that was said by the birds, and by every living creature. When he got back to his sheep he found the flock grazing peacefully, and as he was very tired he laid himself down by them to rest a little. Hardly had he done so when two ravens flew down and perched on a tree near by, and began to talk to each other in their own language: "If that shepherd only knew that there is a vault full of gold and silver beneath where that lamb is lying, what would he not do?" When the shepherd heard these words he went straight to his master and

told him, and the master at once took a wagon, and broke open the door of the vault, and they carried off the treasure. But instead of keeping it for himself, the master, who was an honourable man, gave it all up to the shepherd, saying: "Take it, it is yours. The gods have given it to you." So the shepherd took the treasure and built himself a house. He married a wife, and they lived in great peace and happiness, and he was acknowledged to be the richest man, not only in his native village, but of all the country-side. He had flocks of sheep, and cattle, and horses without end, as well as beautiful clothes and jewels.

One day, just before Christmas, he said to his wife: "Prepare everything for a great feast; to-morrow we will take things with us to the farm that the shepherds there may make merry." The wife obeyed, and all was prepared as he desired. Next day they both went to the farm, and in the evening the master said to the shepherds: "Now come, all of you, eat, drink, and make merry. I will watch the flocks myself to-night in your stead." Then he went out to spend the night with the flocks.

When midnight struck the wolves howled and the dogs barked, and the wolves spoke in their own tongue, saying: "Shall we come in and work havoc, and you too shall eat flesh?" And the dogs answered in their tongue: "Come in, and for once we shall have enough to eat."

Now amongst the dogs there was one so old that he had only two teeth left in his head, and he spoke to the wolves, saying: "So long as I have my two teeth still in my head, I will let no harm be done to my master."

All this the master heard and understood, and as soon as morning dawned he ordered all the dogs to be killed excepting the old dog. The farm servants wondered at this order, and exclaimed: "But surely, sir, that would be a pity!"

The master answered: "Do as I bid you"; and made ready to return home with his wife, and they mounted their horses, her steed being a mare." As they went on their way, it happened that the husband rode on ahead, while the wife was a little way behind. The husband's horse, seeing this, neighed, and said to the mare: "Come along, make haste; why are you so slow?" And the mare answered: "It is very easy for you. You carry only your master, who is a thin man, but I carry my mistress, who is so fat that she weighs as much as three." When the husband heard that, he looked back and laughed, which the wife perceiving, she urged on the mare till she caught up with her husband, and asked him why he laughed. "For nothing at all," he answered; "just because it came into my head."

She would not be satisfied with this answer, and urged him more and more to tell her why he had laughed. But he controlled himself and said: "Let me be, wife; what ails you? I do not know myself why I laughed." But the more he put her off, the more she tormented him to tell her the cause of his laughter. At length he said to her: "Know, then, that if I tell it you I shall immediately and surely die." But even this did not quiet her; she only besought him the more to tell her. Meanwhile they had reached home, and before getting down from his horse the man called for a coffin to be

61

brought; and when it was there he placed it in front of the house, and said to his wife:

"See, I will lay myself down in this coffin, and will then tell you why I laughed, for as soon as I have told you I shall surely die." So he lay down in the coffin, and while he took a last look around him, his old dog came out from the farm and sat down by him, and whined. When the master saw this, he called to his wife: "Bring a piece of bread to give to the dog." The wife brought some bread and threw it to the dog, but he would not look at it. Then the farm cock came and pecked at the bread; but the dog said to it: "Wretched glutton, you can eat like that when you

see that your master is dying?" The cock answered: "Let him die, if he is so stupid. I have a hundred wives, which I call together when I find a grain of corn, and as soon as they are there I swallow it myself; should one of them dare to be angry, I would give her a lesson with my beak. He has only one wife, and he cannot keep her in order."

As soon as the man understood this, he got up out of the coffin, seized a stick, and called his wife into the room, saying: "Come, and I will tell you what you so much want to know"; and then he began to beat her with the stick, saying with each blow: "It is that, wife, it is that!" And in this way he taught her never again to ask why he had laughed.

*Immovable stubbornness is
the keynote of the next two stories.
In one story a shepherd refuses to say a required phrase;
in the other a prime minister insists on repeating
something which endangers his life.
In both cases, the fixed determination brings
unexpected rewards.*

To Your Good Health!

EDITED BY ANDREW LANG

Illustrated by DENVER GILLEN

LONG, long ago there lived a king who was such a mighty monarch that whenever he sneezed everyone in the whole country had to say "To your good health!" Everyone said it except the shepherd with the staring eyes, and he would not say it.

The king heard of this and was very angry, and sent for the shepherd to appear before him.

The shepherd came and stood before the throne, where the king sat looking very grand and powerful. But however grand or powerful he might be the shepherd did not feel a bit afraid of him.

"Say at once, 'To my good health!'" cried the king.

"To my good health!" replied the shepherd.

"To mine—to *mine*, you rascal, you vagabond!" stormed the king.

"To mine, to *mine*, your Majesty," was the answer.

"But to *mine*—to my own," roared the king, and beat on his breast in a rage.

"Well, yes; to mine, of course, to my own," cried the shepherd, and gently tapped his breast.

The king was beside himself with fury and did not know what to do, when the Lord Chamberlain interfered:

"Say at once—say this very moment: 'To your health, your Majesty'; for if you don't say it you'll lose your life," whispered he.

"No, I won't say it till I get the princess for my wife," was the shepherd's answer. Now the princess was sitting on a little throne beside the king, her father, and she looked as sweet and lovely as a little golden dove. When she heard what the shepherd said she could not help laughing, for there is no denying the fact that this young shepherd with the staring eyes pleased her very much; indeed he pleased her better than any king's son she had yet seen.

But the king was not as pleasant as his daughter, and he gave orders to throw the shepherd into the white bear's pit.

The guards led him away and thrust him into the pit with the white bear, who had had nothing to eat for two days and was very hungry. The door of the pit was hardly closed when the bear rushed at the shepherd; but when it saw his eyes it was so frightened that it was ready to eat itself. It shrank away into a corner and gazed at him from there, and, in spite of being so famished, did not dare to touch him, but sucked its own paws from sheer hunger. The shepherd felt that if he once removed his eyes off the beast he was a dead man. In order to keep himself awake he made songs and sang them, and so the night went by.

Next morning the Lord Chamberlain came to see the shepherd's bones, and was amazed to find him alive and well. He led him to the king, who fell into a furious passion, and said: "Well, you have learned what it is to be very near death, and *now* will you say 'To my good health'?"

65

66

But the shepherd answered: "I am not afraid of ten deaths! I will only say it if I may have the princess for my wife."

"Then go to your death," cried the king; and ordered him to be thrown into the den with the wild boars. The wild boars had not been fed for a week, and when the shepherd was thrust into their den they rushed at him to tear him to pieces. But the shepherd took a little flute out of the sleeve of his jacket and began to play a merry tune, on which the wild boars first of all shrank shyly away, and then got up on their hind legs and danced gaily. The shepherd would have given anything to be able to laugh, they looked so funny; but he dared not stop playing, for he knew well enough that the moment he stopped they would fall upon him and tear him to pieces. His eyes were of no use to him here, for he could not have stared ten wild boars in the face at once; so he kept on playing, and the wild boars danced very slowly, as if in a minuet, then by degrees he played faster and faster till they could hardly twist and turn quickly enough, and ended by all falling over each other in a heap, quite exhausted and out of breath. Then the shepherd ventured to laugh at last; and he laughed so long and so loud that when the Lord Chamberlain came early in the morning, expecting to find only his bones, the tears were still running down his cheeks from laughter.

As soon as the king was dressed the shepherd was again brought before him; but he was more angry than ever to think the wild boars had not torn the man to bits, and he said: "Well, you have learned what it feels to be near ten deaths, *now* say 'To my good health!' "

But the shepherd broke in with, "I do not fear a hundred deaths, and I will only say it if I may have the princess for my wife."

"Then go to a hundred deaths!" roared the king, and ordered the shepherd to be thrown down the deep vault of scythes.

The guards dragged him away to a dark dungeon, in the middle of which was a deep well with sharp scythes all round it. At the bottom of the well was a little light by which one could see if anyone was thrown in whether he had fallen to the bottom.

When the shepherd was dragged to the dungeons he begged the guards to leave him alone a little while that he might look down into the pit of scythes; perhaps he might after all make up his mind to say 'To your good health' to the king. So the guards left him alone and he stuck up his long stick near the well, hung his cloak round the stick and put his hat on the top. He also hung his knapsack up inside the cloak so that it might seem to have some body within it. When this was done he called out to the guards and said that he had considered the matter but after all he could not make up his mind to say what the king wished. The guards came in, threw the hat and cloak, knapsack, and stick all down the well together, watched to see how they put out the light at the bottom, and came away, thinking that now there really was an end of the shepherd. But he had hidden in a dark corner and was laughing to himself all the time.

Quite early next morning came the Lord Chamberlain, carrying a lamp and he nearly fell backwards with surprise when he saw the shepherd alive and

well. He brought him to the king, whose fury was greater than ever, but who cried:

"Well, now you have been near a hundred deaths; will you say: 'To your good health'?"

The shepherd gave the same answer:

"I won't say it till the princess is my wife."

"Perhaps after all you may do it for less," said the king, who saw that there was no chance of making away with the shepherd; and he ordered the state coach to be got ready; then he made the shepherd get in with him and sit beside him, and ordered the coachman to drive to the silver wood. When they reached it he said: "Do you see this wood? Well, if you will say, 'To your good health,' I will give it to you."

The shepherd turned hot and cold by turns, but he still persisted:

"I will not say it till the princess is my wife."

The king was much vexed; he drove further on till they came to a splendid castle, all of gold, and then he said:

"Do you see this golden castle? Well, I will give you that too, the silver wood and the golden castle, if only you will say that one thing to me: 'To your good health.'"

The shepherd gaped and was quite dazzled, but he still said:

"No, I will *not* say it till I have the princess for my wife."

This time the king was overwhelmed with grief, and gave orders to drive on to the diamond pond, and there he tried once more.

"Do you see this diamond pond? I will give you that too, the silver wood and the golden castle and the diamond pond. You shall have them all—all—if you will but say: 'To your good health!'"

The shepherd had to shut his staring eyes tight not to be dazzled with the brilliant pond, but still he said:

68

"No, no; I will not say it till I have the princess for my wife."

Then the king saw that all his efforts were useless, and that he might as well give in, so he said:

"Well, well, it's all the same to me—I will give you my daughter to wife; but, then, you really and truly must say to me: 'To your good health.'"

"Of course I'll say it; why should I not say it? It stands to reason that I shall say it then."

At this the king was more delighted than anyone could have believed. He made it known all through the country that there were to be great rejoicings, as the princess was going to be married. And everyone rejoiced to think that the princess, who had refused so many royal suitors, should have ended by falling in love with the staring-eyed shepherd.

There was such a wedding as had never been seen. Everyone ate and drank and danced. Even the sick were feasted, and quite tiny new-born children had presents given them.

But the greatest merry-making was in the king's palace; there the best bands played and the best food was cooked; a crowd of people sat down to table, and all was fun and merry-making.

And when the groomsman, according to custom, brought in the great boar's head on a big dish and placed it before the king so that he might carve it and give everyone a share, the savoury smell was so strong that the king began to sneeze with all his might.

"To your very good health," cried the shepherd before anyone else, and the king was so delighted that he did not regret having given him his daughter.

In time, when the old king died, the shepherd succeeded him. He made a very good king and never expected his people to wish him well against their wills; but, all the same, everyone did wish him well, for they all loved him.

69

The Thanksgiving of the Wazir

EDITED BY ANDREW LANG

Illustrated by DENVER GILLEN

ONCE upon a time there lived in Hindustan two kings whose countries bordered upon each other; but, as they were rivals in wealth and power, and one was a Hindu rajah and the other a Mohammedan bâdshah, they were not good friends at all. In order, however, to escape continual quarrels, the rajah and the bâdshah had drawn up an agreement, stamped and signed, declaring that if any of their subjects, from the least to the greatest, crossed the boundary between the two kingdoms, he might be seized and punished.

One morning the bâdshah and his chief wazir, or prime minister, were just about to begin their morning's work over the affairs of the kingdom, and the bâd-

shah had taken up a pen and was cutting it to his liking with a sharp knife, when the knife slipped and cut off the tip of his finger.

"Oh-he, wazir!" cried the king, "I've cut the tip of my finger off!"

"That is good hearing!" said the wazir in answer.

"Insolent one," exclaimed the king. "Do you take pleasure in the misfortunes of others, and in mine also? Take him away, my guards, and put him in the court prison until I have time to punish him as he deserves!"

Instantly the officers in attendance seized upon the luckless wazir, and dragged him out of the king's presence towards the narrow doorway through

70

which unhappy criminals were wont to be led to prison or execution. As the door opened to receive him, the wazir muttered something into his great white beard which the soldiers could not hear.

"What said the rascal?" shouted the angry king.

"He says, he thanks your majesty," replied one of the gaolers. And at his words, the king stared at the closing door, in anger and amazement.

"He must be mad," he cried, "for he is grateful, not only for the misfortunes of others, but for his own; surely something has turned his head!"

Now the king was very fond of his old wazir, and although the court physician came and bound up his injured finger with cool and healing ointment, and soothed the pain, he could not soothe the soreness of the king's heart, nor could any of all his ministers and courtiers, who found his majesty very cross all the day long.

Early next morning the king ordered his horse and declared that he would go hunting. Instantly all was bustle and preparation in stable and hall, and by the time he was ready a score of ministers and huntsmen stood ready to mount and accompany him; but to their astonishment the king would have none of them. Indeed, he glared at them so fiercely that they were glad to leave him. So away and away he wandered, over field and through forest, so moody and thoughtful that many a fat buck and gaudy pheasant escaped without notice, and so careless was he whither he was going that he strayed without perceiving it over into the rajah's territory, and only discovered the fact when, suddenly,

men stepped from all sides out of a thicket, and there was nothing left but surrender. Then the poor bâdshah was seized and bound and taken to the rajah's prison, thinking most of the time of his wazir, who was suffering a similar fate, and wishing that, like the wazir, he could feel that there was something to give thanks for.

That night the rajah held a special council to consider what should be done to his rival who had thus given himself into his hands. All the Brahmans were sent for—fat priests who understood all about everything, and what days were lucky and what unlucky—and, whilst all the rest of the rajah's councillors were offering him different advice until he was nearly crazy with anger and indecision, the chief Brahman was squatting in a corner figuring out sums and signs to himself with an admiring group of lesser priests around him. At last he arose, and advanced towards the throne.

"Well," said the rajah anxiously, "what have you to advise?"

"A very unlucky day!" exclaimed the chief Brahman. "Oh, a very unlucky day! The god Devi is full of wrath, and commands that to-morrow you must chop off this bâdshah's head and offer it in to him in sacrifice."

"Ah, well," said the rajah, "let it be done. I leave it to you to carry out the sentence." And he bowed to the priests and left the room.

Before dawn great preparations were being made for a grand festival in honour of the great idol Devi. Hundreds of banners waved, hundreds of drummers drummed, hundred of singers chanted chants, hundreds of priests, well washed and anointed, performed their sacred rites, whilst the rajah sat, nervous and ill at ease, amongst hundreds of courtiers and servants, wishing it were all well over. At last the time came for the sacrifice to be offered, and the poor bâdshah was led out bound, to have his head chopped off.

The chief Brahman came along with a smile on his face, and a big sword in his hand, when, suddenly, he noticed that the bâdshah's finger was tied up in a bit of rag. Instantly he dropped the sword, and, with his eyes starting out of his head with excitement, pounced upon the rag and tore it off, and there he saw that the tip of his victim's finger was missing. At this he got very red and angry indeed, and he led the bâdshah up to where the rajah sat wondering.

"Behold! O rajah," he said, "this sacrifice is useless; the tip of his finger is gone! A sacrifice is no sacrifice unless it is complete." And he began to weep with rage and mortification.

But of instead of wailing likewise, the rajah gave a sigh of relief, and answered: "Well, that settles the matter. If it had been anyone else I should not have minded; but, somehow—a king and all—well, it doesn't seem quite right to sacrifice a king." And with that he jumped up and with his jewelled dagger cut the bâdshah's cords, and marched with him out of the temple back to the palace.

After having bathed and refreshed his guest, the rajah loaded him with gifts, and himself accompanied him with a large escort as far as the frontier between their kingdoms, where, amidst salutes and great rejoicings, they tore up the old agreement and drew up another in which each king promised welcome and safe conduct to any of the other's people, from the least to the greatest, who came over the border on any errand whatever. And so they embraced, and each went his own way.

When the bâdshah got home that very evening he sent for his imprisoned wazir.

"Well, O wazir!" he said, when the old man had been brought before him, "what think you has been happening to me?"

"How can a man in prison know what is happening outside it?" answered the wazir.

Then the bâdshah told him all his adventures. And when he had reached the end he added:

"I have made up my mind, as a token of gratitude for my escape, to pardon you freely, if you will tell me why you gave thanks when I cut off the tip of my finger."

"Sire," replied the old wazir, "am I not right in thinking that it was a very lucky thing for you that you *did* cut off the tip of your finger, for otherwise you would certainly have lost your head. And to lose a scrap of one's finger is surely the least of the two evils."

"Very true," answered the king, touching his head as he spoke, as if to make quite certain that it was still there, "but yet—why did you likewise give thanks when I put you into prison?"

"I gave thanks," said the wazir, "because it is good always to give thanks. And had I known that my being in prison was to prevent the god Devi claiming me instead of your majesty, as a perfect offering, I should have given greater thanks still."

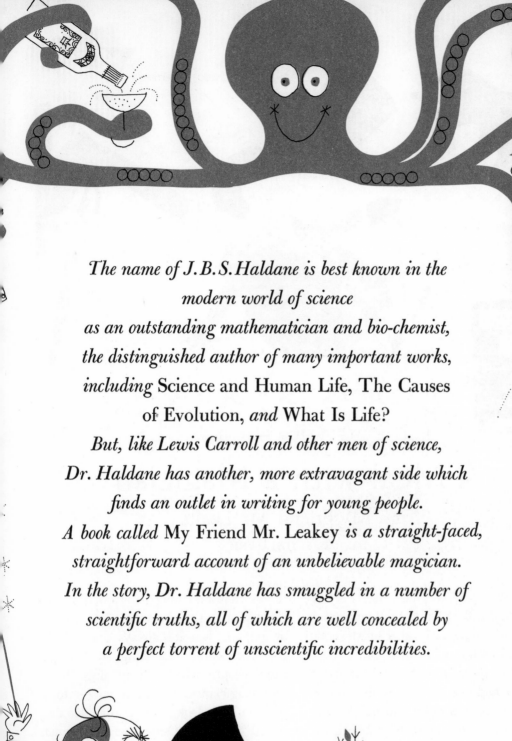

*The name of J.B.S.Haldane is best known in the
modern world of science
as an outstanding mathematician and bio-chemist,
the distinguished author of many important works,
including* Science and Human Life, The Causes
of Evolution, *and* What Is Life?
*But, like Lewis Carroll and other men of science,
Dr. Haldane has another, more extravagant side which
finds an outlet in writing for young people.
A book called* My Friend Mr. Leakey *is a straight-faced,
straightforward account of an unbelievable magician.
In the story, Dr. Haldane has smuggled in a number of
scientific truths, all of which are well concealed by
a perfect torrent of unscientific incredibilities.*

73

A Meal with a Magician

From My Friend Mr. Leakey

BY J. B. S. HALDANE
Illustrated by FRANK DANIEL

I HAVE HAD some very odd meals in my time, and if I liked I could tell you about a meal in a mine, or a meal in Moscow, or a meal with a millionaire. But I think you will be more interested to hear about a meal I had one evening with a magician, because it is more unusual. People don't often have a meal of that sort, for rather few people know a magician at all well, because there aren't very many in England. Of course I am talking about real magicians. Some conjurors call themselves magicians, and they are very clever men. But they can't do the sort of

things that real magicians do. I mean, a conjuror can turn a rabbit into a bowl of goldfish, but it's always done under cover or behind something, so that you can't see just what is happening. But a real magician can turn a cow into a grandfather clock with people looking on all the time. Only it is very much harder work, and no one could do it twice a day, and six days a week, like the conjurors do with rabbits.

When I first met Mr. Leakey I never guessed he was a magician. I met him like this: I was going across the Haymarket about five o'clock one afternoon. When I got to the refuge by a lamp-post in the middle I stopped, but a little man who had crossed so far with me went on. Then he saw a motor-bus going down the hill and jumped back, which is always a silly thing to do. He jumped right in front of a car, and if I hadn't grabbed his overcoat collar and pulled him back on to the refuge, I think the car would have knocked him down. For it was wet weather, and the road was very greasy, so it only skidded when the driver put the brakes on.

The little man was very grateful, but dreadfully frightened, so I gave him my arm across the street, and saw him back to his home, which was quite near. I won't tell you where it was, because if I did you might go there and bother him, and if he got really grumpy it might be very awkward indeed for you. I mean, he might make one of your ears as big as a cabbage-leaf, or turn your hair green, or exchange your right and left feet, or something like that. And then everyone who saw you would burst out laughing, and say, "Here comes wonky Willie, or lopsided Lissie," or whatever your name is.

"I can't bear modern traffic," he said, "the motor-buses make me so frightened. If it wasn't for my work in London I should like to live on a little island where there are no roads, or on the top of a mountain, or somewhere like that." The little man was sure I had saved his life, and insisted on my having dinner with him, so I said I would come to dinner on Wednesday week. I didn't notice anything specially odd about him then, except that his ears were rather

large and that he had a little tuft of hair on the top of each of them, rather like the lynx at the Zoo. I remember I thought if I had hair there I would shave it off. He told me that his name was Leakey, and that he lived on the first floor.

Well, on Wednesday week I went to dinner with him. I went upstairs in a block of flats and knocked at a quite ordinary door, and the little hall of the flat was quite ordinary too, but when I got inside it was one of the oddest rooms I have ever seen. Instead of wallpaper there were curtains round it, embroidered with pictures of people and animals. There was a picture of two men building a house, and another of a man with a dog and a cross-bow hunting rabbits. I know they were made of embroidery, because I touched them, but it must have been a very funny sort of embroidery, because the pictures were always changing. As long as you looked at them they stayed still, but if you looked away and back again they had altered. During dinner the builders had put a fresh storey on the house, the hunter had shot a bird with his cross-bow, and his dog had caught two rabbits.

The furniture was very funny too. There was a bookcase made out of what looked like glass with the largest books in it that I ever saw, none of them less than a foot high, and bound in leather. There were cupboards running along the tops of the bookshelves. The chairs were beautifully carved, with high wooden backs, and there were two tables. One was made of copper, and had a huge crystal globe on it. The other was a solid lump of wood about ten feet long, four feet wide, and three feet high, with holes cut in it so that you could get your knees under it. There were various odd things hanging from the ceiling. At first I couldn't make out how the room was lit. Then I saw that the light came from plants of a sort I had never seen before, growing in pots. They had red, yellow and blue fruits about as big as tomatoes, which shone. They weren't disguised electric lamps, for I touched one and it was quite cold, and soft like a fruit.

"Well," said Mr. Leakey, "what would you like for dinner?"

"Oh, whatever you've got," I said.

"You can have whatever you like," he said. "Please choose a soup."

So I thought he probably got his dinner from a restaurant, and I said, "I'll have Bortsch," which is a red Russian soup with cream in it.

"Right," he said, "I'll get it ready. Look here, do you mind if we have dinner served the way mine usually is? You aren't easily frightened, are you?"

"Not very easily," I said.

"All right, then, I'll call my servant, but I warn you he's rather odd."

76

At that Mr. Leakey flapped the tops and lobes of his ears against his head. It made a noise like when one claps one's hands, but not so loud. Out of a large copper pot about as big as the copper you wash clothes in, which was standing in one corner, came what at first I thought was, a large wet snake. Then I saw it had suckers all down one side, and was really the arm of an octopus. This arm opened a cupboard and pulled out a large towel with which it wiped the next arm that came out. The dry arm then clung on to the wall with its suckers, and gradually the whole beast came out, dried itself, and crawled up the wall. It was the biggest octopus I have ever seen; each arm was about eight feet long, and its body was as big as a sack. It crawled up the wall, and then along the ceiling, holding on by its suckers like a fly. When it got above the table it held on by one arm only, and with the other seven got plates and knives and forks out of the cupboards above the bookshelves and laid the table with them.

"That's my servant Oliver," said Mr. Leakey. "He's much better than a person, because he has more arms to work with, and he can hold on to a plate with about ten suckers, so he never drops one."

When Oliver the octopus had laid the table we sat down and he offered me a choice of water, lemonade, beer, and four different kinds of wine with his seven free arms, each of which held a different bottle. I chose some water and some very good red wine from Burgundy.

All this was so odd that I was not surprised to notice that my host was wearing a top hat, but I certainly did think it a little queer when he took it off and poured two platefuls of soup out of it.

"Ah, we want some cream," he added. "Come here, Phyllis." At this a small green cow, about the size of a rabbit, ran out of a hutch, jumped on to the table, and stood in front of Mr. Leakey, who milked her into a silver cream jug which Oliver had handed down for the purpose. The cream was excellent, and I enjoyed the soup very much.

"What would you like next?" said Mr. Leakey.

"I leave it to you," I answered.

"All right," he said, "we'll have grilled turbot, and turkey to follow. Catch us a turbot, please, Oliver, and be ready to grill it, Pompey."

At this Oliver picked up a fishhook with the end of one of his arms and began making casts in the air like a fly-fisher. Meanwhile I heard a noise in the fireplace, and Pompey came out. He was a small dragon about a foot long, not counting his tail, which measured another foot. He had been lying on the burning coals, and was red-hot. So I was glad to see that as soon as he got out of the fire he put a pair of asbestos boots which were lying in the fender on to his hind feet.

"Now, Pompey," said Mr. Leakey, "hold your tail up properly. If you burn the carpet again, I'll pour a bucket of cold water over you. (Of course I wouldn't really do that, it's very cruel to pour cold water onto a dragon, especially a little one with a thin skin)," he added in a low voice, which only I could hear. But poor Pompey took the threat quite seriously. He whimpered, and the yellow flames which were coming out of his nose turned a dull blue. He waddled along rather clumsily on his hind legs, holding up his tail and the front part of his body. I think the asbestos boots made walking rather difficult for him, though they saved the carpet, and no doubt kept his hind feet warm. But of course dragons generally walk on all four feet and seldom wear boots, so I was surprised that Pompey walked as well as he did.

I was so busy watching Pompey that I never saw how Oliver caught the turbot, and by the time I looked up at him again he had just finished cleaning it, and threw it down to Pompey. Pompey caught it in his front paws, which had cooled down a bit, and were just about the right temperature for grilling things. He had long thin fingers with claws on the ends; and held the fish on each hand alternately, holding the other against his red-hot chest to warm it. By the time he had finished and put the grilled fish on to a plate which Oliver handed down Pompey was clearly feeling the cold, for his teeth were chattering, and he scampered back to the fire with evident joy.

"Yes," said Mr. Leakey, "I know some people say it is cruel to let a young dragon cool down like that, and liable to give it a bad cold. But I say a dragon can't begin to learn too soon that life isn't all fire and flames, and the world is a colder place than he'd like it to be. And they don't get colds if you give them plenty of sulphur to eat. Of course a dragon with a cold is an awful nuisance to itself and everyone else. I've known one throw flames for a hundred yards when it sneezed. But that was a full-grown one, of course. It burned down one of the Emperor of China's palaces. Besides, I really couldn't afford to keep a dragon if I didn't make use of him. Last week, for example, I used his breath to burn the old paint off the door, and his tail makes quite a good soldering iron. Then he's really much more reliable than a dog for dealing with burglars. They might shoot a dog, but leaden bullets just melt the moment they touch Pompey. Anyway, I think dragons were meant for use, but not for ornament. Don't you?"

"Well, do you know," I answered, "I am ashamed to say that Pompey is the first live dragon I've ever seen."

"Of course," said Mr. Leakey, "how stupid of me. I have so few guests here except professional colleagues that I forgot you were a layman. By the way," he went on, as he poured sauce out of his hat over the fish, "I don't know if you've noticed anything queer about this dinner. Of course some people are more observant than others."

"Well," I answered, "I've never seen anything like it before."

For example, at that moment I was admiring an enormous rainbow-coloured beetle which was crawling towards me over the table with a salt-cellar strapped on its back.

"Ah well then," said my host, "perhaps you have guessed that I'm a magician. Pompey, of course, is a real dragon, but most of the other animals here were people before I made them what they are now. Take Oliver, for example. When he was a man he had his legs cut off by a railway train. I couldn't stick them on again because my magic doesn't work

against machinery. Poor Oliver was bleeding to death, so I thought the only way to save his life was to turn him into some animal with no legs. Then he wouldn't have any legs to have been cut off. I turned him into a snail, and took him home in my pocket. But whenever I tried to turn him back into something more interesting, like a dog, it had no hind legs. But an octopus has really got no legs. Those eight tentacles grow out of its head. So when I turned him into an octopus, he was all right. And he had been a waiter when he was a man, so he soon learnt his job. I think he's much better than a maid because he can lift the plates from above, and doesn't stand behind one and breathe down one's neck. You may have the rest of the

fish, Oliver, and a bottle of beer. I know that's what you like."

Oliver seized the fish in one of his arms and put it into an immense beak like a parrot's but much bigger, which lay in the centre of the eight arms. Then he took a bottle of beer out of a cupboard, unscrewed the cork with his beak, hoisted himself up to the ceiling with two of his other arms, and turned over so that his mouth was upwards. As he emptied the bottle he winked one of his enormous eyes. Then I felt sure he must be really a man, for I never saw an ordinary octopus wink.

The turkey came in a more ordinary way. Oliver let down a large hot plate, and then a dish cover on to it. There was nothing in the cover, as I could see. Mr.

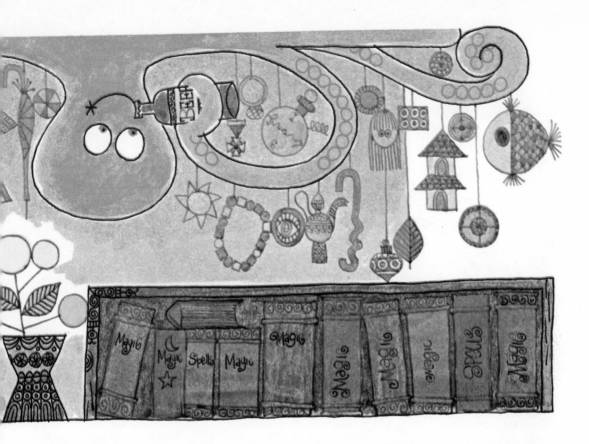

Leakey got up, took a large wand out of the umbrella stand, pointed it at the dish cover, said a few words, and there was the turkey steaming hot when Oliver lifted the cover off it.

"Of course that's easy," said Mr. Leakey, "any good conjuror could do it, but you can never be sure the food you get in that way is absolutely fresh. That's why I like to see my fish caught. But birds are all the better for being a few days old. Ah, we shall want some sausages too. That's easy."

He took a small clay pipe out of his pocket and blew into it. A large brown bubble came out of the other end, shaped like a sausage. Oliver picked it off with the end of one of his tentacles, and put it on a hot plate, and it was a sausage, because I ate it. He made six sausages in

this way, and while I was watching him Oliver had handed down the vegetables. I don't know where he got them. The sauce and gravy came out of Mr. Leakey's hat, as usual.

Just after this the only accident of the evening happened. The beetle who carried the salt-cellar round tripped over a fold in the tablecloth and spilled the salt just in front of Mr. Leakey, who spoke to him very angrily.

"It's lucky for you, Leopold, that I'm a sensible man. If I were superstitious, which I'm not, I should think I was going to have bad luck. But it's you who are going to have bad luck, if anyone. I've a good mind to turn you back into a man, and if I do, I'll put you straight on to that carpet and send you to the nearest police station; and when the

81

police ask you where you've been hiding, d'you think they'll believe you when you say you've been a beetle for the last year? Are you sorry?"

Leopold, with a great struggle, got out of his harness and rolled on to his back, feebly waving his legs in the air like a dog does when he's ashamed of himself.

"When Leopold was a man," said Mr. Leakey, "he made money by swindling people. When the police found it out and were going to arrest him, he came to me for help, but I thought it served him right. So I said, 'If they catch you, you'll get sent to penal servitude for seven years. If you like I'll turn you into a beetle for five years, which isn't so long, and then, if you've been a good beetle, I'll make you into a man with a different sort of face, so the police won't know you.' So now Leopold is a beetle. Well, I see he's sorry for spilling the salt. Now, Leopold, you must pick up all the salt you've spilt."

He turned Leopold over on his front and I watched him begin to pick the salt up. It took him over an hour. First he picked it up a grain at a time in his mouth, lifted himself up on his front legs, and dropped it into the salt-cellar. Then he thought of a better plan. He was a beetle of the kind whose feelers are short and spread out into a fan. He started shovelling the salt with his feelers, and got on much quicker that way. But fairly soon he got uncomfortable. His feelers started to itch or something, and he had to wipe them with his legs. Finally he got a bit of paper, and used it for a shovel, holding it with his front feet.

"That's very clever for a beetle," said my host. "When I turn him back into a man he'll be quite good with his hands, and I expect he'll be able to earn his living at an honest job."

As we were finishing the turkey, Mr. Leakey looked up anxiously from time to time.

"I hope Abdu'l Makkar won't be late with the strawberries," he said.

"Strawberries?" I asked in amazement, for it was the middle of January.

"Oh yes, I've sent Abdu'l Makkar, who is a jinn, to New Zealand for some. Of course it's summer there. He oughtn't to be long now, if he has been good, but you know what jinns are, they have their faults, like the rest of us. Curiosity, especially. When one sends them on long errands they will fly too high. They like to get up quite close to Heaven to overhear what the angels are saying, and then the angels throw shooting stars at them. Then they drop their parcels, or come home half scorched. He ought to be back soon, he's been away over an hour. Meanwhile we'll have some other fruit, in case he's late."

He got up, and tapped the four corners of the table with his wand. At each corner the wood swelled; then it cracked, and a little green shoot came out and started growing. In a minute they were already about a foot high, with several leaves at the top, and the bottom quite woody. I could see from the leaves that one was a cherry, another a pear, and the third a peach, but I didn't know the fourth.

As Oliver was clearing away the remains of the turkey with four of his arms and helping himself to sausage with a fifth, Abdu'l Makkar came in. He came feet first through the ceiling, which seemed to close behind him like water in the tank of the diving birds' house in the Zoo, when you look at it from underneath while a penguin dives in. It shook a little for a moment afterwards. He narrowly missed one of Oliver's arms, but alighted safely on the floor, bending his knees to break his fall, and bowing deeply to Mr. Leakey. He had a brown face with rather a long nose, and looked quite like a man, except that he had a pair of leathery wings folded on his back, and his nails were of gold. He wore a turban and clothes of green silk.

"Oh peacock of the world and redresser of injustices," he said, "thy unworthy servant comes into the presence with rare and refreshing fruit."

"The presence deigns to express gratification at the result of thy labours."

"The joy of thy negligible slave is as the joy of King Solomon, son of David (on whom be peace, if he has not already obtained peace) when he first beheld Balkis, the queen of Sheba. May the Terminator of delights and Separator of companions be far from this dwelling."

"May the Deluder of Intelligences never trouble the profundity of thine apprehension."

"Oh dominator of demons and governor of goblins, what egregious enchanter or noble necromancer graces thy board?"

"It is written, oh Abdu'l Makkar, in the book of the sayings of the prophet Shoaib, the apostle of the Midianites, that curiosity slew the cat of Pharaoh, king of Egypt."

"That is a true word."

"Thy departure is permitted. Awaken me at the accustomed hour. But stay!

*This is, of course, a gross exaggeration.

My safety razor hath no more blades and the shops of London are closed. Fly therefore to Montreal, where it is even now high noon, and purchase me a packet thereof."

"I tremble and obey."

"Why dost thou tremble, oh audacious among the Ifreets?"

"Oh Emperor of enchantment, the lower air is full of aeroplanes, flying swifter than a magic carpet,* and each making a din like unto the bursting of the great dam of Sheba, and the upper air is infested with meteorites."

"Fly therefore at a height of five miles and thou shalt avoid both the one peril and the other. And now, oh performer of commands and executor of behests, thou hast my leave to depart."

"May the wisdom of Plato, the longevity of Shiqq, the wealth of Solomon, and the success of Alexander, be thine."

"The like unto thee, with brazen knobs thereon."

The jinn now vanished, this time through the floor. While he and Mr. Leakey had been talking the trees had grown up to about four feet high, and flowered. The flowers were now falling off, and little green fruits were swelling.

"You have to talk like that to a jinn or you lose his respect. I hope you don't mind my not introducing you, but really jinns may be quite awkward at times," said my host. "Of course Abdu'l Makkar is a nice chap and means well, but he might be very embarrassing to you, as you don't know the Word of Power to send him away. For instance, if you were playing cricket and went in against a fast bowler, he'd probably turn up and ask you 'Shall I slay thine enemy, oh

Defender of the Stumps, or merely convert him into an he-goat of loathsome appearance and afflicted with the mange?' You know, I used to be very fond of watching cricket, but I can't do it now. Quite a little magic will upset a match. Last year I went to see the Australians playing against Gloucester, and just because I felt a little sympathetic with Gloucestershire the Australian wickets went down like ninepins. If I hadn't left before the end they'd have been beaten. And after that I couldn't go to any of the test matches. After all, one wants the best side to win."

We next ate the New Zealand strawberries, which were very good, with Phyllis's cream. While we did so Pompey, who acted as a sort of walking stove, came out again and melted some cheese to make a Welsh rarebit. After this we went on to dessert. The fruit was now quite ripe. The fourth tree bore half a dozen beautiful golden fruits shaped rather like apricots, but much bigger, and my host told me they were mangoes, which of course usually grow in India. In fact you can't make them grow in England except by magic. So I said I would try a mango.

"Aha," said Mr. Leakey, "this is where I have a pull over Lord Melchett or the Duke of Westminster, or any other rich man. They might be able to get mangoes here by aeroplane, but they couldn't give them as dessert at a smart dinner-party."

"Why not?" I asked.

"That shows you've never eaten one. The only proper place to eat a mango is in your bath. You see, it has a tough skin and a squashy inside, so when once you

get through the skin all the juice squirts out. And that would make a nasty mess of people's white shirts. D'you ever wear a stiff-fronted shirt?"

"Not often."

"A good thing too. You probably don't know why people wear them. It's a curious story. About a hundred years ago a great Mexican enchanter called Whiz-

topacoatl came over to Europe. And he got very annoyed with the rich men. He didn't so much mind their being rich, but he thought they spent their money on such ugly things, and were dreadfully stodgy and smug. So he decided to turn them all into turtles. Now to do that somebody has to say two different spells at the same time, which is pretty diffi-

cult, I can tell you. So Whiztopacoatl went round to an English sorcerer called Mr. Benedict Barnacle, to borrow a two-headed parrot that belonged to him. It was rather like one of those two-headed eagles they used to have on the Russian and Austrian flags. Then he was going to teach one of the heads one spell, and the other head the second spell; and when the parrot said both at once all the rich men would have turned into turtles. But Mr. Barnacle persuaded him to be less fierce, so finally they agreed that for a hundred years the rich men in Europe should be made to wear clothes only fit for turtles. Because of course the front of a turtle is stiff and flat, and it is the only sort of animal that would be quite comfortable in a shirt with a stiff flat front. They made a spell to stiffen all the shirts, and of course it worked very well, but it's wearing off now, and soon nobody will wear such silly clothes anymore.

"About your mango; you can eat it quite safely, if you just wait a moment while I enchant it so that it won't splash over you."

Quite a short spell and a little wiggling of his wand were enough, and then I ate the mango. It was wonderful. It was the only fruit I have ever eaten that was better than the best strawberries. I can't describe the flavour, which is a mixture of all sorts of things, including a little resin, like the smell of a pine forest in summer. There is a huge flattish stone in the middle, too big to get into your mouth, and all round it a squashy yellow pulp. To test the spell I tried to spill some down my waistcoat, but it merely jumped up into my mouth. Mr. Leakey ate a pear, and gave me the other five mangoes to take home. But I had to eat them in my bath because they weren't enchanted.

While we were having coffee (out of the hat, of course) Mr. Leakey rubbed one corner of the table with his wand and it began to sprout with very fine green grass. When it was about as high as the grass on a lawn, he called Phyllis out of her hutch, and she ate some of it for her dinner. We talked for a while about magic, football, and the odder sorts of dog, such as Bedlington terriers and rough-haired Dachshunds, and then I said I must be getting home.

"I'll take you home," said Mr. Leakey, "but when you have a day to spare you must come round and spend it with me, if you'd care to see the sort of things I generally do, and we might go over to India or Java or somewhere for the afternoon. Let me know when you're free. But now just stand on this carpet, and shut your eyes, because people often get giddy the first two or three times they travel by magic carpet."

We got on to the carpet. I took a last look at the table, where Leopold had just finished picking up the salt, and was resting, while Phyllis was chewing the cud. Then I shut my eyes, my host told the carpet my address, flapped his ears, and I felt a rush of cold air on my cheeks, and a slight giddiness. Then the air was warm again. Mr. Leakey told me to open my eyes, and I was in my sitting-room at home, five miles away. As the room is small, and there were a number of books and things on the floor, the carpet could not settle down properly, and stayed about a foot up in the air. Luckily it was quite stiff, so I stepped down off it, and turned the light on.

"Good-night," said Mr. Leakey, bending down to shake my hand, and then he flapped his ears and he and the carpet vanished. I was left in my room with nothing but a nice full feeling and a parcel of mangoes to persuade me that I had not been dreaming.

The stories known as **The Arabian Nights**
are supposed to have been told by a queen named Scheherazade
in order to save her life. Her husband, the king,
had been deceived by his first wife and had vowed
to marry another womau every night and have her killed
the very next morning. On her wedding night,
Scheherazade began to tell the king a story,
but did not finish it.
The king was so eager to hear
the end of it that he postponed her execution.
The second night, Scheherazade finished the story
and began a second one, which she also left uncompleted.
This she cleverly continued to do for one thousand and one nights
—the collection is sometimes called
"The Book of the Thousand Nights and One Night"
—at the end of which time the king
was so delighted with her that he never
again referred to his fatal vow.
"The Story of the Enchanted Horse"
is one of the least known but most
marvelous of these stories.

The Story of the Enchanted Horse

From The Arabian Nights

Illustrated by ROBERT J. LEE

ON THE FESTIVAL of the Nooroze, which is the first day of the year and of spring, the Sultan of Shiraz was just concluding his public audience, when a Hindu appeared at the foot of the throne with an artificial horse, so spiritedly modeled that at first sight he was taken for a living animal.

The Hindu prostrated himself before the throne, and pointing to the horse, said to the Sultan, "This horse is a great wonder; if I wish to be transported to the most distant parts of the earth, I have only to mount him. I offer to show your Majesty this wonder if you command me."

The Sultan, who was very fond of everything that was curious, and who had never beheld or heard anything quite so strange as this, told the Hindu that he would like to see him perform what he had promised.

The Hindu at once put his foot into the stirrup, swung himself into the saddle, and asked the Sultan whither he wished him to go.

"Do you see yonder mountain?" said the Sultan, pointing to it. "Ride your horse there, and bring me a branch from the palm tree that grows at the foot of the hill."

No sooner had the Sultan spoken than the Hindu turned a peg, which was in the hollow of the horse's neck, just by the pommel of the saddle. Instantly the horse rose from the ground, and bore his rider into the air with the speed of lightning, to the amazement of the Sultan and all the spectators. Within less than a quarter of an hour they saw him returning with the palm branch in his hand. Alighting amidst the acclamations of the people, he dismounted and, approaching the throne, laid the palm branch at the Sultan's feet.

The Sultan, still marveling at this unheard-of sight, was filled with a great desire to possess the horse, and said to the Hindu, "I will buy him of you, if he is for sale."

"Sire," replied the Hindu, "there is only one condition on which I will part with my horse, namely, the hand of the Princess, your daugher, as my wife."

The courtiers surrounding the Sultan's throne could not restrain their laughter at the Hindu's extravagant proposal. But Prince Feroze Shah, the Sultan's eldest son, was very indignant. "Sire," said he, "I hope that you will at once refuse this impudent demand, and not allow this miserable juggler to flatter himself for a moment with the hope of a marriage with one of the most powerful houses in the world. Think what you owe to yourself and to your noble blood!"

"My son," replied the Sultan, "I will not grant him what he asks. But putting my daughter the Princess out of the question, I may make a different bargain with him. First, however, I wish you to examine the horse; try him yourself, and tell me what you think of him."

On hearing this the Hindu eagerly ran forward to help the Prince mount, and show him how to guide and manage the horse. But without waiting for the Hindu's assistance, the Prince mounted and turned the peg as he had seen the other do. Instantly the horse darted into the air, swift as an arrow shot from a bow; and in a few moments neither horse nor Prince could be seen. The Hindu, alarmed at what had happened, threw himself before the throne and begged the Sultan not to be angry.

"Your Majesty," he said, "saw as well as I with what speed the horse flew away. The surprise took away my power of speech. But even if I could have spoken to advise him, he was already too far away to hear me. There is still room to hope, however, that the Prince will discover that there is another peg, and as soon as he turns that, the horse will cease to rise, and will descend gently to the ground."

Notwithstanding these arguments the Sultan was much alarmed at his son's evident danger, and said to the Hindu, "Your head shall answer for my son's life, unless he returns safe in three months' time, or unless I hear that he is alive." He then ordered his officers to secure the Hindu and keep him a close prisoner; after which he retired to his palace, sorrowing that the Festival of Nooroze had ended so unluckily.

Meanwhile, the Prince was carried through the air with fearful rapidity. In less than an hour he had mounted so high that the mountains and plains below him all seemed to melt together. Then for the first time he began to think of returning, and to this end he began turning the peg, first one way and then the other, at the

90

same time pulling upon the bridle. But when he found that the horse continued to ascend he was greatly alarmed, and deeply repented of his folly in not learning to guide the horse before he mounted. He now began to examine the horse's head and neck very carefully, and discovered behind the right ear a second peg, smaller than the first. He turned this peg and presently felt that he was descending in the same oblique manner as he had mounted, but not so swiftly.

Night was already approaching when the Prince discovered and turned the small peg; and as the horse descended he gradually lost sight of the sun's last setting rays, until presently it was quite dark. He was obliged to let the bridle hang loose, and wait patiently for the horse to choose his own landing place, whether it might be in the desert, in the river or in the sea.

At last, about midnight, the horse stopped upon solid ground, and the Prince dismounted, faint with hunger, for he had eaten nothing since the morning. He found himself on the terrace of a magnificent palace; and groping about, he presently reached a staircase which led down into an apartment, the door of which was half open.

The Prince stopped and listened at the door, then advanced cautiously into the room, and by the light of a lamp saw a number of black slaves, sleeping with their naked swords beside them. This was evidently the guard chamber of some Sultan or Princess. Advancing on tiptoe, he drew aside the curtain and saw a magnificent chamber, containing many beds, one of which was placed higher than the others on a raised dais—evidently the beds of the Princess and her women. He crept softly toward the dais, and beheld a beauty so extraordinary that he was charmed at the first sight. He fell on his knees and gently twitched the sleeve of the Princess, who opened her eyes and was greatly surprised to see a handsome young man bending over her, yet showed no sign of fear. The Prince rose to his feet, and, bowing to the ground, said:

"Beautiful Princess, through a most extraordinary adventure you see at your feet a suppliant Prince, son of the Sultan of Persia, who prays for your assistance and protection."

In answer to this appeal of Prince Feroze Shah, the beautiful Princess said:

"Prince, you are not in a barbarous country, but in the kingdom of the Rajah of Bengal. This is his country estate, and I am his eldest daughter. I grant you the protection that you ask, and you may depend upon my word."

The Prince of Persia would have thanked the Princess, but she would not let him speak. "Impatient though I am," said she, "to know by what miracle you have come here from the capital of Persia, and by what enchantment you escaped the watchfulness of my guards, yet I will restrain my curiosity until later, after you have rested from your fatigue."

The Princess' women were much surprised to see a Prince in her bedchamber, but they at once prepared to obey her command, and conducted him into a handsome apartment. Here, while some prepared the bed, others brought and served a welcome and bountiful supper.

The next day the Princess prepared to receive the Prince, and took more pains in dressing and adorning herself than she ever had done before. She decked her neck, head and arms with the finest diamonds she possessed, and clothed herself in the richest fabric of the Indies, of a most beautiful color, and made only for Kings, Princes and Princesses. After once more consulting her glass, she sent word to the Prince of Persia that she would receive him.

The Prince, who had just finished dressing when he received the Princess' message, hastened to avail himself of the honor conferred on him. He told her of the wonders of the Enchanted Horse, of his wonderful journey through the air, and of the means by which he had gained entrance to her chamber. Then, after thanking her for her kind reception, he expressed a wish to return home and relieve the anxiety of the Sultan his father. The Princess replied, "I cannot approve, Prince, of your leaving so soon. Grant me the favor of a somewhat longer visit, so that you may take back to the court of Persia a better account of what you have seen in the Kingdom of Bengal."

The Prince could not well refuse the Princess this favor, after the kindness she had shown him; and she busied herself with plans for hunting parties, concerts and magnificent feasts to render his stay agreeable.

For two whole months the Prince of Persia abandoned himself entirely to the will of the Princess, who seemed to think that he had nothing to do but pass his whole life with her. But at last he declared that he could stay no longer, and begged leave to return to his father.

"And, Princess," he added, "if I were not afraid of giving offense, I would ask the favor of taking you along with me."

The Princess made no answer to this address of the Prince of Persia; but her silence and downcast eyes told him plainly that she had no reluctance to accompany him. Her only fear, she confessed, was that the Prince might not know well enough how to govern the horse. But the Prince soon removed her fear by assuring her that after the experience he had had, he defied the Hindu himself to manage the horse better. Accordingly they gave all their thoughts to planning how to get away secretly from the palace, without anyone having a suspicion of their design.

The next morning, a little before daybreak, when all the attendants were still asleep, they made their way to the terrace of the palace. The Prince turned the horse toward Persia, and as soon as the Princess had mounted behind him and was well settled with her arms about his waist, he turned the peg, whereupon the horse mounted into the air with his accustomed speed, and in two hours' time they came in sight of the Persian capital.

Instead of alighting at the palace, the Prince directed his course to a kiosk a little distance outside the city. He led the Princess into a handsome apartment, ordered the attendants to provide her with whatever she needed, and told her that he would return immediately after informing his father of their arrival. Thereupon he ordered a horse to be brought and set out for the palace.

The Sultan received his son with tears of joy, and listened eagerly while the Prince related his adventures during his flight through the air, his kind reception at the palace of the Princess of Bengal, and his long stay there due to their mutu-

al affection. He added that, having promised to marry her, he had persuaded her to accompany him to Persia. "I brought her with me on the Enchanted Horse," he concluded, "and left her in your summer palace till I could return and assure her of your consent."

Upon hearing these words, the Sultan embraced his son a second time, and said to him, "My son, I not only consent to your marriage with the Princess of Bengal, but will myself go and bring her to the palace, and your wedding shall be celebrated this very day."

The Sultan now ordered that the Hindu should be released from prison and brought before him. When this was done, the Sultan said, "I held you prisoner that your life might answer for that of the Prince my son. Thanks be to God, he has returned in safety. Go, take your horse, and never let me see your face again."

The Hindu had learned of those who brought him from prison, all about the Princess whom Prince Feroze Shah had brought with him and left at the kiosk,

and at once he began to think of revenge. He mounted his horse and flew directly to the kiosk, where he told the Captain of the Guard that he came with orders to conduct the Princess of Bengal through the air to the Sultan, who awaited her in the great square of his palace.

The Captain of the Guard, seeing that the Hindu had been released from prison, believed his story. And the Princess at once consented to do what the Prince, as she thought, desired of her.

The Hindu, overjoyed at the ease with which his wicked plan was succeeding, mounted his horse, took the Princess up behind him, turned the peg, and instantly the horse mounted into the air.

Meanwhile, the Sultan of Persia, attended by his court, was on the road to the kiosk where the Princess of Bengal had been left, while the Prince himself had hurried on ahead to prepare the Princess to receive his father. Suddenly the Hindu, to brave them both, and avenge himself for the ill-treatment he had received, appeared over their heads with his prize.

When the Sultan saw the Hindu, his surprise and anger were all the more keen because it was out of his power to punish his outrageous act. He could only stand and hurl a thousand maledictions at him, as did also the courtiers who had witnessed this unequaled piece of insolence. But the grief of Prince Feroze Shah was indescribable, when he beheld the Hindu bearing away the Princess who he loved so passionately. He made his way, melancholy and brokenhearted, to the kiosk where he had last taken leave of the Princess. Here, the Captain of the Guard, who had already learned of the Hindu's treachery, threw himself at the Prince's feet, and condemned himself to die by his own hand, because of his fatal credulity.

"Rise," said the Prince, "I blame, not you, but my own want of precaution, for the loss of my Princess. But lose no time,

bring me a dervish's robe, and take care that you give no hint that it is for me."

When the Captain of the Guard had procured the dervish's robe, the Prince at once disguised himself in it, and taking with him a box of jewels, left the palace, resolved not to return until he had found his Princess or perish in the attempt.

Meanwhile, the Hindu, mounted on his Enchanted Horse, with the Princess behind him, arrived at the capital of the Kingdom of Cashmere. He did not enter the city, but alighted in a wood, and left the Princess on a grassy spot close to a rivulet of fresh water, while he went to seek food. On his return, and after he and the Princess had partaken of refreshment, he began to maltreat the Princess, because she refused to become his wife.

Now it happened that the Sultan of

94

Cashmere and his court were passing through the wood on their return from hunting, and hearing a woman's voice calling for help, went to her rescue. The Hindu with great impudence asked what business anyone had to interfere, since the lady was his wife! Whereupon the Princess cried out:

"My Lord, whoever you are whom Heaven has sent to my assistance, have compassion on me! I am a Princess. This Hindu is a wicked magician who has forced me away from the Prince of Persia, whom I was to marry, and has brought me hither on the Enchanted Horse that you see there."

The Princess' beauty, majestic air, and tears all declared that she spoke the truth. Justly enraged at the Hindu's insolence, the Sultan of Cashmere ordered his guards to seize him and strike off his head, which sentence was immediately carried out.

The Princess' joy was unbounded at finding herself rescued from the wicked Hindu. She supposed that the Sultan of Cashmere would at once restore her to the Prince of Persia, but she was much deceived in these hopes. For her rescuer had resolved to marry her himself the next day, and issued a proclamation commanding the general rejoicing of the inhabitants.

The Princess of Bengal was awakened at break of day by drums and trumpets and sounds of joy throughout the palace, but was far from guessing the true cause. When the Sultan came to wait upon her, he explained that these rejoicings were in honor of their marriage, and begged her to consent to the union. On hearing this the Princess fainted away.

95

The serving-women who were present ran to her assistance, but it was long before they could bring her back to consciousness. When at last she recovered, she resolved that sooner than be forced to marry the Sultan of Cashmere she would pretend that she had gone mad. Accordingly she began to talk wildly, and show other signs of a disordered mind, even springing from her seat as if to attack the Sultan, so that he became greatly alarmed and sent for all the court physicians to ask if they could cure her of her disease.

When he found that his court physicians could not cure her, he sent for the most famous doctors in his kingdom, who had no better success. Next, he sent word to the courts of neighboring Sultans with promises of generous reward to anyone who could cure her malady. Physicians arrived from all parts, and tried their skill, but none could boast of success.

Meanwhile, Prince Feroze Shah, disguised as a dervish, traveled through many provinces and towns, everywhere inquiring about his lost Princess. At last in a certain city of Hindustan he learned of a Princess of Bengal who had gone mad on the day of her intended marriage with the Sultan of Cashmere. Convinced that there could be but one Princess of Bengal, he hastened to the capital of Cashmere and upon arriving was told the story of the Princess, and the fate of the Hindu magician. The Prince was now convinced that he had at last found the beloved object of his long search.

Providing himself with the distinctive dress of a physician, he went boldly to the palace and announced his wish to be allowed to attempt the cure of the Princess. Since it was now some time since any physician had offered himself, the Sultan had begun to lose hope of ever seeing the

Princess cured, though he still wished to marry her. So he at once ordered the new physician to be brought before him; and upon the Prince being admitted, told him that the Princess could not bear the sight of a physician without falling into the most violent paroxysms. Accordingly he conducted the Prince to a closet from which he might see her through a lattice without himself being seen. There Feroze Shah beheld his lovely Princess sitting in hopeless sorrow, the tears flowing from her beautiful eyes, while she sang a plaintive air deploring her unhappy fate. Upon leaving the closet, the Prince told the Sultan that he had assured himself that the Princess' complaint was not incurable, but that if he was to aid her he must speak with her in private and alone.

The Sultan ordered the Princess' chamber door to be opened, and Feroze Shah went in. Immediately the Princess resorted to her old practice of meeting physicians with threats, and indications of attacking them. But Feroze Shah came close to her and said in so low a voice that only she could hear, "Princess, I am not a physician, but Feroze Shah, and have come to obtain your liberty."

The Princess, who knew the sound of his voice, and recognized him, notwithstanding he had let his beard grow so long, grew calm at once, and was filled with secret joy at the unexpected sight of the Prince she loved. After they had briefly informed each other of all that had happened since their separation, the Prince asked if she knew what had become of the horse after the death of the Hindu magician. She replied that she did not know, but supposed that he was carefully guarded as a curiosity. Feroze Shah

then told the Princess that he intended to obtain and use the horse to convey them both back to Persia; and they planned together, as the first step to this end, that the Princess the next day should receive the Sultan.

On the following day the Sultan was overjoyed to find that the Princess' cure was apparently far advanced, and regarded the Prince as the greatest physician in the world. The Prince of Persia, who accompanied the Sultan on his visit to the Princess, inquired of him how she had come into the Kingdom of Cashmere from her far-distant country.

The Sultan then repeated the story of the Hindu magician, adding that the Enchanted Horse was kept safely in his treasury as a great curiosity, though he knew not how to use it.

"Sire," replied the pretended physician, "this information affords me a means of curing the Princess. When she was brought hither on the Enchanted Horse, she contracted part of the enchantment, which can be dispelled only by a certain incense of which I have knowledge. Let the horse be brought tomorrow into the great square before the palace, and leave the rest to me. I promise to show you and all your assembled people, in a few moments' time, the Princess of Bengal completely restored in body and mind. But to assure the success of what I propose, the Princess must be dressed as magnificently as possible and adorned with the most valuable jewels in your treasury."

All this the Sultan eagerly promised, for he would have undertaken far more difficult things to assure his marriage with the Princess.

The next day the Enchanted Horse was

taken from the treasury and brought to the great square before the palace. The rumor of something extraordinary having spread through the town, crowds of people flocked thither from all sides. The Sultan of Cashmere, surrounded by his nobles and ministers of state, occupied a gallery erected for the purpose. The Princess of Bengal, attended by her ladies in waiting, went up to the Enchanted Horse, and the women helped her to mount. The pretended physician then placed around the horse many vessels full of burning charcoal, into which he cast handfuls of incense. After which, he ran three times about the horse, pretending to utter certain magic words. The pots sent forth a dark cloud of smoke that surrounded the Princess, so that neither she nor the horse could be seen. The Prince mounted nimbly behind her and turned the peg; and as the horse rose with them into the air, the Sultan distinctly heard these words, "Sultan of Cashmere, when you would marry Princesses who implore your protection, learn first to obtain their consent!"

Thus the Prince delivered the Princess of Bengal, and carried her that same day to the capital of Persia where the Sultan his father made immediate preparation for the solemnization of their marriage with all fitting pomp and magnificence. After the days appointed for rejoicing were over, the Sultan named and appointed an ambassador to go to the Rajah of Bengal, to ask his approval of the alliance contracted by this marriage; which the Rajah of Bengal took as an honor, and granted with great pleasure and satisfaction.

The next eight stories
form a collection within a collection.
They come from eight different countries
and carry the color and spirit
of foreign lands.
"The Flower Elves" is from China,
"Grasp All, Lose All" is from India,
"Simpleton Peter" from England, "Sadko the Minstrel"
from Russia, "The Prince of the Seven Golden Cows"
from France.
"The Good Housewife and Her Night Helpers" from Scotland,
"The Water-Sprite and the Bear" from Germany,
and "The Man with the Bag" from Ireland.
These tales are told by various skilled writers;
the last is by the Irish-American
poet Padraic Colum.

The Flower Elves

Illustrated by FRANK DANIEL

ONCE UPON a time there was a scholar who lived retired from the world in order to gain hidden wisdom. He lived alone and in a secret place. And all about the house in which he dwelt he had planted every kind of flower, and bamboos and other trees. There it lay, quite concealed in its thick grove of flowers. With him he had only a boy servant, who dwelt in a separate hut, and who carried out his orders. He was not allowed to appear before his master unless summoned. The

scholar loved his flowers as he did himself. Never did he set his foot beyond the boundaries of his garden.

It chanced that once there came a lovely spring evening. Flowers and trees stood in full bloom, a fresh breeze was blowing, the moon shone clearly. And the scholar sat over his goblet and was grateful for the gift of life.

Suddenly he saw a maiden in dark garments come tripping up in the moonlight. She made a deep curtsey, greeted him and said: "I am your neighbor. We are a company of young maids who are on our way to visit the eighteen aunts. We should like to rest in this court for awhile, and therefore ask your permission to do so."

The scholar saw that this was something quite out of the common, and gladly gave his consent. The maiden thanked him and went away.

In a short time she brought back a whole crowd of maids carrying flowers and willow branches. All greeted the scholar. They were charming with delicate features, and slender, graceful figures. When they moved their sleeves, a delightful fragrance was exhaled. There is no fragrance known to the human world which could be compared with it.

The scholar invited them to sit down for a time in his room. Then he asked them: "Whom have I really the honor of entertaining? Have you come from the castle of the Lady in the Moon, or the Jade Spring of the Queen-Mother of the West?"

"How could we claim such high descent?" said a maiden in a green gown, with a smile. "My name is Salix." Then she presented another, clad in white, and said: "This is Mistress Prunophora"; then one in rose, "and this is Persica"; and finally one in a dark-red gown, "and this is Punica." We are all sisters and we want to visit the eighteen zephyr-aunts to-day. The moon shines so beautifully this evening and it is so charming here in the garden. We are most grateful to you for taking pity on us."

"Yes, yes," said the scholar.

Then their plainly-clad servants suddenly announced: "The zephyr-aunts have already arrived!"

At once the girls rose and went to the door to meet them.

"We were just about to visit you, aunts," they said, smiling. "This gentleman here had just invited us to sit for a moment. What a pleasant coincidence that you have come here, too. This is such a lovely night that we must drink a goblet of nectar in honor of our aunts!"

Thereupon they ordered their servants to bring what was needed.

"May one sit down here?" asked the aunts.

"The master of the house is most kind," replied the maids, "and the spot is quiet and hidden."

And then they presented the aunts to the scholar. He spoke a few kindly words to the eighteen aunts. They had a somewhat unsettled and airy manner. Their words fairly gushed out, and in their neighborhood one felt a frosty chill.

Meanwhile the servants had already brought in table and chairs. The eighteen aunts sat at the upper end of the board, the maids followed, and the scholar sat down with them at the lowest place. Soon the entire table was covered with the most delicious foods and most magnificent fruits, and the goblets were filled with a fragrant nectar. They were delights such as the world of men does not know! The moon shone brightly and the flowers exhaled intoxicating odors. After they had partaken of food and drink the maids rose, danced and sung. Sweetly the sound of their singing echoed through the falling dusk, and their dance was like that of butterflies fluttering about the flowers. The scholar was so overpowered that he no longer knew whether he were in heaven or on earth.

When the dance had ended, the girls sat down again at the table, and drank the health of their aunts in flowing nectar. The scholar, too, was remembered with a toast, to which he replied with well-turned phrases.

But the eighteen aunts were somewhat irresponsible in their ways. One of them, raising her goblet, by accident poured some nectar on Punica's dress. Punica, who was young and fiery, and very neat, stood up angrily when she saw the spot on her red dress.

"You are really very careless," said she, in her anger. "My other sisters may be afraid of you, but I am not!"

Then the aunts grew angry as well and said: "How dare this young chit insult us in such a manner!"

And with that they gathered up their garments and rose.

All the maids then crowded about them and said: "Punica is so young and inexperienced! You must not bear her any ill-will! To-morrow she shall go to you switch in hand, and receive her punishment!"

But the eighteen aunts would not listen to them and went off. Thereupon the maids also said farewell, scattered among the flower-beds and disappeared. The scholar sat for a long time lost in dreamy yearning.

On the following evening the maids all came back again.

"We all live in your garden," they told him. "Every year we are tormented by naughty winds, and therefore we have always asked the eighteen aunts to protect us. But yesterday Punica insulted them, and now we fear they will help us no more. But we know that you have always been well disposed toward us, for which we are heartily grateful. And now we have a great favor to ask, that every New Year's day you make a small scarlet flag, paint the sun, moon and five planets on it, and set it up in the eastern part of the garden. Then we sisters will be left in peace and will be protected from all evil. But since New Year's day has passed for this year, we beg that you will set up the flag on the twenty-first of this month. For the East Wind is coming and the flag will protect us against him!"

The scholar readily promised to do as they wished, and the maids all said with a single voice: "We thank you for your great kindness and will repay it!" Then they departed and a sweet fragrance filled the entire garden.

The scholar, however, made a red flag as described, and when early in the morn-ing of the day in question the East Wind really did begin to blow, he quickly set it up in the garden.

Suddenly a wild storm broke out, one that caused the forests to bend, and broke the trees. The flowers in the garden alone did not move.

Then the scholar noticed that Salix was the willow; Prunophora the plum; Persica the peach, and the saucy Punica the pomegranate, whose powerful blossoms the wind cannot tear. The eighteen zephyr-aunts, however, were the spirits of the winds.

In the evening the flower-elves all came and brought the scholar radiant flowers as a gift of thanks.

"You have saved us," they said, "and we have nothing else we can give you. If you eat these flowers you will live long and avoid old age. And if you will protect us this way every year, then we sisters, too, will live long."

The scholar did as they told him and ate the flowers. And his figure changed and he grew young again like a youth of twenty.

And in the course of time he attained the hidden wisdom and was placed among the Immortals.

Grasp All, Lose All

EDITED BY ANDREW LANG
Illustrated by FRANK DANIEL

ONCE, in former times, there lived in a certain city in India a poor oil-seller, called Déna, who never could keep any money in his pockets; and when this story begins he had borrowed from a banker, of the name of Léna, the sum of one hundred rupees; which, with the interest Léna always charged, amounted to a debt of three hundred rupees. Now Déna was doing a very bad business, and had no money with which to pay his debt, so Léna was very angry, and used to come round to Déna's house every evening and abuse him until the poor man was nearly worried out of his life. Léna generally fixed his visit just when

Déna's wife was cooking the evening meal, and would make such a scene that the poor oil-seller and his wife and daughter quite lost their appetites, and could eat nothing. This went on for some weeks, till, one day, Déna said to himself that he could stand it no longer, and that he had better run away; and, as a man cannot fly easily with a wife and daughter, he thought he must leave them behind. So that evening, instead of turning into his house as usual after his day's work, he just slipped out of the city without knowing very well where he was going.

At about ten o'clock that night Déna

105

came to a well by the wayside, near which grew a giant peepul tree; and, as he was very tired, he determined to climb it, and rest for a little before continuing his journey in the morning. Up he went and curled himself so comfortably amongst the great branches that, overcome with weariness, he fell fast asleep. Whilst he slept, some spirits, who roam about such places on certain nights, picked up the tree and flew away with it to a far-away shore where no creature lived, and there, long before the sun rose, they set it down. Just then the oil-seller awoke; but instead of finding himself in the midst of a forest, he was amazed to behold nothing but waste shore and wide sea, and was dumb with horror and astonishment. Whilst he sat up, trying to collect his senses, he began to catch sight here and there of twinkling, flashing lights, like little fires, that moved and sparkled all about, and wondered what they were. Presently he saw one so close to him that he reached out his hand and grasped it, and found that it was a sparkling red stone, scarcely smaller than a walnut. He opened a corner of his loin-cloth and tied the stone in it; and by-and-by he got another, and then a third, and a fourth, all of which he tied up carefully in his cloth. At last, just as the day was breaking, the tree rose, and, flying rapidly through the air, was deposited once more by the well where it had stood the previous evening.

When Déna had recovered a little from the fright which the extraordinary antics of the tree had caused him, he began to thank Providence that he was alive, and, as his love of wandering had been quite cured, he made his way back to the city and to his own house. Here he was met and soundly scolded by his wife, who assailed him with a hundred questions and reproaches. As soon as she paused for breath, Déna replied:

"I have only this one thing to say, just look what I have got!" And, after carefully shutting all the doors, he opened the corner of his loin-cloth and showed her the four stones, which glittered and flashed as he turned them over and over.

"Pooh!" said his wife, "the silly pebbles! If it was something to eat, now, there'd be some sense in them; but what's the good of *such* things?" And she turned away with a sniff, for it had happened that the night before, when Léna had come round as usual to storm at Déna, he had been rather disturbed to find that his victim was from home, and had frightened the poor woman by his threats. Directly, however, he heard that Déna had come back, Léna appeared in the doorway. For some minutes he talked to the oil-seller at the top of his voice, until he was tired, then Déna said:

"If your honour would deign to walk into my humble dwelling, I will speak."

So Léna walked in, and the other, shutting as before all the doors, untied the corner of his loin-cloth and showed him the four great flashing stones.

"This is all," said he, "that I have in the world to set against my debt, for, as your honour knows, I haven't a penny, but the stones are pretty!"

Now Léna looked and saw at once that these were magnificent rubies, and his mouth watered for them; but as it would never do to show what was in his mind, he went on:

"What do I care about your stupid stones? It is my money I want, my lawful debt which you owe me, and I shall get it out of you yet somehow or another, or it will be the worst for you."

To all his reproaches Déna could answer nothing, but sat with his hands joined together beseechingly, asking for patience and pity. At length Léna pretended that, rather than have a bad debt on his hand, he would be at the loss of taking the stones in lieu of his money; and, whilst Déna nearly wept with gratitude, he wrote out a receipt for the three hundred rupees; and, wrapping the four stones in a cloth, he put them into his bosom, and went off to his house.

"How shall I turn these rubies into money?" thought Léna, as he walked along; "I daren't keep them, for they are of great value, and if the rajah heard that I had them he would probably put me into prison on some pretence and seize the stones and all else that I have as well. But what a bargain I have got! Four rubies worth a king's ransom, for one hundred rupees! Well, well, I must take heed not to betray my secret." And he went on making plans. Presently he made up his mind what to do, and, putting on his cleanest clothes, he set off to the house of the chief wazir, whose name was Musli, and, after seeking a private audience, he brought out the four rubies and laid them before him.

The wazir's eyes sparkled as he beheld the splendid gems.

"Fine, indeed," murmured he. "I can't buy them at their real value; but, if you like to take it, I will give you ten thousand rupees for the four."

To this the banker consented grate-fully; and handing over the stones in exchange for the rupees, he hurried home, thanking his stars that he had driven such a reasonable bargain and obtained such an enormous profit.

After Léna had departed the wazir began casting about in his mind what to do with the gems; and very soon determined that the best thing to do was to present them to the rajah, whose name was Kahré. Without losing a moment, he went that very day to the palace, and sought a private interview with the rajah; and when he found himself alone with his royal master, he brought the four jewels and laid them before him.

"Oh, ho!" said the rajah, "these are priceless gems, and you have done well to give them to me. In return I give you and your heirs the revenues of ten villages."

Now the wazir was overjoyed at these words, but only made his deepest obeisance; and, whilst the king put the rubies into his turban, hurried away beaming with happiness at the thought that for ten thousand rupees he had become lord of ten villages. The rajah was also equally pleased, and strolled off with his new purchases to the women's quarters and showed them to the queen, who was nearly out of her mind with delight. Then, as she turned them over and over in her hands, she said: "Ah! if I had eight more such gems, what a necklace they would make! Get me eight more of them or I shall die!"

"Most unreasonable of women," cried the rajah, "where am I to get eight more such jewels as these? I gave ten villages for them, and yet you are not satisfied!"

"What does it matter?" said the rani;

"do you want me to die? Surely you can get some more where these came from?" And then she fell to weeping and wailing until the rajah promised that in the morning he would make arrangements to get some more such rubies, and that if she would be patient she should have her desire.

In the morning the rajah sent for the wazir, and said that he must manage to get eight more rubies like those he had brought him the day before, "and if you don't I shall hang you," cried the rajah, for he was very cross. The poor wazir protested in vain that he knew not where to seek them; his master would not listen to a word he said.

"You *must,*" said he; "the rani shall not die for the want of a few rubies! Get more where those came from."

The wazir left the palace, much troubled in mind, and bade his slaves bring Léna before him. "Get me eight more such rubies as those you brought yesterday," commanded the wazir, directly the banker was shown into his presence. "Eight more, and be quick, or I am a dead man."

"But how can I?" wailed Léna; "rubies like those don't grow upon bushes!"

"Where did you get them from?" asked the wazir.

"From Déna, the oil-seller," said the banker.

"Well, send for him and ask him where *he* got them," answered the wazir. "I am not going to hang for twenty Dénas!" And more slaves were sent to summon Déna.

When Déna arrived he was closely questioned, and then all three started to see the rajah, and to him Déna told the whole story.

"What night was it that you slept in the peepul tree?" demanded the rajah.

"I can't remember," said Déna; "but my wife will know."

Then Déna's wife was sent for, and she explained that it was on the last Sunday of the new moon.

Now everyone knows that it is on the Sunday of the new moon that spirits have special power to play pranks upon mortals. So the rajah forbade them all, on pain of death, to say a word to anyone; and declared that, on the next Sunday of the new moon, they four—Kahré, Musli, Léna, and Déna—would go and sit in the peepul tree and see what happened.

The days dragged on to the appointed Sunday, and that evening the four met secretly, and entered the forest. They had not far to go before they reached the peepul tree, into which they climbed as the rajah had planned. At midnight the tree began to sway, and presently it moved through the air.

"See, sire," whispered Déna, "the tree is flying!"

"Yes, yes," said the rajah, "you have told the truth. Now sit quiet, and we shall see what happens."

Away and away flew the tree with the four men clinging tightly to its branches, until at last it was set down by the waste sea-shore where a great wide sea came tumbling in on a desert beach. Presently, as before, they began to see little points of light that glistened like fires all around them. Then Déna thought to himself, "Think! last time I only took four that came close to me, and I got rid of all my debt in return. This time I will take all I can get and be rich!"

"If I got ten thousand rupees for four stones," thought Léna, "I will gather forty now for myself, and become so wealthy that they will probably make me a wazir at least!"

"For four stones I received ten villages," Musli was silently thinking; "now I will get stones enough to purchase a kingdom, become a rajah, and employ wazirs of my own!"

And Kahré thought: "What is the good of only getting eight stones? Why, here are enough to make twenty necklaces; and wealth means power!"

Full of avarice and desire, each scrambled down from the tree, spread his cloth, and darted hither and thither picking up the precious jewels, looking the while over his shoulder to see whether his neighbour fared better than he. So engrossed were they in the business of gathering wealth that the dawn came upon them unawares; and suddenly the tree rose up again and flew away, leaving them upon the sea-shore staring after it, each with his cloth heavy with priceless jewels.

Morning broke in the city, and great was the consternation in the palace when the chamberlains declared that the rajah had gone out the evening before and had not returned.

"Ah!" said one, "it is all right! Musli wazir will know where he is, for it was he who was the king's companion."

Then they went to the wazir's house, and there they learnt that the wazir had left it the evening before and had not returned. "But," said a servant, "Léna the banker will know where he is, for it was with him that Musli went."

Then they visited the house of Léna, and there they learnt that the banker had gone out the evening before, and that he too had not returned; but the porter told them that he was accompanied by Déna the oil-seller, so he would know where they were.

So they departed to Déna's house, and Déna's wife met them with a torrent of reproaches and wailings, for Déna too had gone off the evening before to Léna's house and had not returned.

In vain they waited, and searched—never did any of the hapless four return to their homes; and the confused tale which was told by Déna's wife was the only clue to their fate.

To this day, in that country, when a greedy man has overreached himself, and lost all in grasping at too much, folks say:

"All has he lost!—neither Déna, nor Léna, nor Musli, nor Kahré remain." And not five men in a hundred know how the proverb began, nor what it really signifies.

110

Simpleton Peter

RETOLD BY JAMES REEVES
Illustrated by LILIAN OBLIGADO

THERE WAS once a young man called Peter, who lived in a country village with his old widowed mother. He was a good-hearted fellow, tall and strong, but he was one of the simplest of men ever born. He could scarcely count his mother's hens, though she had only a score; if he spent threepence out of a shilling, he hardly knew how to work out the change; and as for going to market, he never went without being cheated. It was not for want of trying; it was not because he was lazy; it was just that poor Peter seemed to have been born with scarcely any brains in his head.

"Oh, mother," he would say, "if only I'd been given just a wee bit of brains, I'd not be so much trouble and worry to you."

"Ay, Peter," his mother would say, with a sigh, "you're short of brains, there's no doubt, but you're a good boy, and as strong as any other two, so don't you let it worry you. Now run upstairs and get me three buttons to sew on your jacket, and mind you three is three and not two, nor four neither."

All the same, Peter used to fret about his foolishness. So he continued to pester his mother till at last she said:

111

"Well, if you want to come by some brains, just take a walk to the wise woman who lives on the hill. She's a right clever body, they say, with her magic books and her pills and potions, and perhaps she can help you."

So when his work was done, Peter walked up the hill, and on the top he found the cottage of the wise woman, with smoke coming out of the chimney and a black cat stretched out asleep in the doorway.

"Well, that's a good sign," said Peter to himself, and knocked at the door.

112

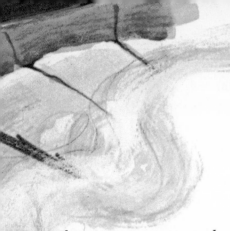

There was no answer, so he lifted the latch cautiously and looked in. There was the old woman, stirring a round black pot on the fire. She neither turned nor said a word, so Peter stepped inside and said:

"Good day to you, wise woman. 'Tis a very fine day, to be sure."

The old woman said nothing, but went on stirring.

"Maybe we shall have rain tomorrow," Peter went on.

But still the old woman said nothing.

"And maybe we shan't," he added, wondering what to say next.

Still the old woman went on stirring.

"Well now," said Peter, "that's all I have to say about the weather, so let's come to business. I'm a very simple fellow, and I came to see whether you could supply me with a wee bit of brains. You see—"

"Brains?" said the old woman, putting down her spoon and turning round for the first time. "Yes, I dare say. That depends on what sort of brains you want. If it's king's brains, or soldier's brains, or schoolmaster's brains, then I can't help you. What sort of brains do you want?"

"Just ordinary brains," said Peter. "Middling good, and middling bad, like most of the folks round here."

"Very good," said the wise woman.

"Such brains you shall have, but you must fetch me the heart of the thing you like above all others. Do you understand? And when you have brought me that, you must answer me a riddle, so that I may tell whether you have really brought the thing I ask for. Now be off with you."

Without waiting for an answer, she took up the pot and carried it into the back kitchen, leaving Peter to let himself out. He went off down the hill, thinking about what the wise woman had said. "The heart of the thing I like above all others," he repeated to himself. "Now what can that be, I wonder?" For this was not the sort of thing Peter usually thought about. When he got home, he told his mother what the old woman had said, and his mother thought the question over. At last she said:

"Why, there's nothing in this world you like better than fat bacon, if you ask me. So we'd best kill the old sow, and you can take its heart to the wise woman."

So the old sow was killed and her heart removed, and Peter took it next evening to the cottage on the hill.

The wise woman was sitting in a chair by the fireplace reading a great book. She scarcely looked up, and Peter put the heart down on the table.

"There 'tis," he said. "The heart of the thing I like best in all the world. Will it do?"

The old woman looked up from her book.

"What is it," she said, "that can run without feet? Tell me that."

"What is it than can run without feet?" repeated the young man, and he scratched his head, and thought and thought till his head ached.

The old woman went on reading. At last Peter spoke.

"I tell you what," he said. "I dunno."

"Well, that's not the thing I asked for," said the old woman. "Take it away and be off with you."

There was nothing for poor Peter to do but pick up the sow's heart and go home again.

When he got near his own cottage, he saw there were people standing about the doorway, and some of the women were crying. Then he learnt that his old widowed mother had been taken suddenly ill and was near death. He went inside the cottage and closed the door. The old woman was indeed very feeble. Peter saw there was nothing to be done, so he knelt by the bedside and took her hand.

"Say good-bye to me, son," she whispered, "for I'm going to leave you. But now you've been to the wise woman and got yourself some brains, you'll be able to look after yourself."

Peter had not the heart to tell her that he had got no brains and had not even been able to answer the wise woman's riddle. Instead, he kissed his mother and said:

"All the same, mother, I shall miss you badly. Good-bye, mother dear, good-bye."

"Good-bye, my son," said the old woman; and with that she closed her eyes, smiled at him faintly, and died.

Peter stayed for a long while kneeling by the bed, crying and crying, for he could not stop the tears from coming. And he thought of all she had done for him—how she had brought him up as a little boy, and healed his cuts when he fell over, and cooked his meals, and mended his clothes, and talked to him, and been company for him in the evenings. He wondered how in the world he would get on without her. "For," he said to himself, "of all creatures in the world, she was the one I liked best."

Then he thought of the wise woman's words.

"Bring me," she had said, "the heart of the one you like best in all the world."

"That I shan't," he said, "not for all the brains on earth."

But next morning he thought he might take his dead mother up to the old woman without taking her heart out, for he was even more in need of a bit of brains than ever. So he put his mother in a sack and took her up the hill. This he did without difficulty, for his mother had been a frail little woman, and he himself was as strong as any two ordinary men. He laid the body down in the wise woman's cottage and said:

"Now this time I have surely brought you the thing I love above all others. Here is my very own dead mother, and now you must give me the brains you promised."

"Tell me this," said the wise woman. "What is it that is yellow and shines and isn't gold?"

"What's it that is yellow and shines and isn't gold?" Peter said.

But he couldn't think of the answer for the life of him, so at last he said:

"I dunno."

"Then you shall get no brains today. You're a simple fellow indeed, and maybe you'll never have any at all."

So Peter took up the sack with his mother inside and went out. But he was too sad to go home; instead, he sat down by the roadside and began to cry.

Presently he heard the sound of a gentle voice at his side. He looked up and saw a handsome young girl watching him with a kindly smile.

"What's the matter?" she asked. "I'm sorry to see a great fellow like you in distress."

"I'm a simple fellow," said Peter, "without any brains, and now my mother has died and left me all alone. So how I'll manage from now on I don't know. There's no one to cook for me and sew for me and manage the marketing, and worst of all, there's no one to talk to me and cheer me up when I'm in trouble."

"I'll help you," said Jenny, for this was the girl's name. "A simple fellow like you shouldn't be without someone to look after him. Will you let me come and look after you?"

"If you like," said Peter, "but you'll find I'm a more than commonly stupid man, unless I can get some brains from somewhere."

"Well," said Jenny, "they say that a foolish man makes the best husband. Will you marry me?"

"Can you cook?" said Peter.

"Yes, indeed," said Jenny.

"Can you sew and mend clothes?"

"To be sure."

"Can you count eggs and add up pounds, shillings, and pence?"

"Well enough."

"Then, if you'll marry me, I'll have you," agreed Peter.

Off they went, and after Peter's mother had been buried and all the village had mourned for her, the two of them were married and made their home together in the cottage. Soon Peter, simple as he was, began to see that he had got a very good wife. She cooked and sewed, mended and washed, all with the greatest cheerfulness and good will. What is more, she kept Peter amused with her witty talk and her gentle ways. Peter was not a bad husband either, for he, too, worked cheerfully and well; nothing was too much trouble for him, so long as he did not have to think; no weight was too much for him to lift, and no distance was too great for him to walk. In short, they were as happy and contented a couple as had ever set up house together in the village.

115

"Why, Jenny," said Peter one evening, "I believe that of all creatures in the world, you're the one I like the best."

And these words put an idea into his head.

"Surely," he went on, "the wise woman didn't mean me to kill you and take her your heart. Do you think she could have meant that, Jenny?"

"I hope not," said his wife, "indeed I do. Who said anything about killing? Why not take me up to her, alive as I am, heart and all?"

"That's a very good notion," said Peter. "Why couldn't I have thought of it myself? Just you come along with me. But first, you'd better see if you can answer riddles. Tell me, what is it that can run without legs?"

"Why, a river, to be sure," said Jenny. "That's not very hard."

"A river?" repeated the simpleton. "Of course. Now why couldn't I have thought of that? But tell me this: what is it that shines and is yellow, but isn't gold?"

"The sun," said Jenny, without stopping to think. "I could have told you that when I was five years old."

"The sun?" said Peter in a puzzled way. "Yes—that shines, to be sure; and 'tis yellow; and 'tisn't gold neither. Why, what a head you have, Jenny! There can't be a man in all England with a cleverer wife than I have. Come along quickly now, and see if the old woman will give me a little bit of brains, so that I can be more your equal."

So they went up the hill together, and found the wise woman at home.

"Wise woman," said Peter, "at last I've brought you the creature I like above all others. Here she is, heart and all. If you don't give me the brains I ask for now, you're no wise woman, but a cheat and a fraud."

"Sit down, both of you," said the old woman. They sat down, and she turned to Peter and said, "Now then, here's my riddle. What is it that has first no legs, then two, then four?"

Poor Peter thought and thought, but the answer would not come; then Jenny whispered in his ear:

"A tadpole. Say 'a tadpole.' "

"A tadpole," said Peter promptly; and the old woman said:

"Right. Now I see you've got all the brains you want, and they are inside your wife's head. If a man has a clever wife, she is all the brains he needs. Now be off with you, and don't come bothering me any more."

Peter and Jenny got up, thanked the old woman, and went on their way.

As they went down the hill, Jenny was singing quietly to herself, but Peter said nothing.

"What are you thinking of?" she asked gently, stopping in the middle of a song.

Peter left off scratching his head and said nothing. At last he turned to her and answered:

"I was only thinking how proud I am to have such a more than commonly clever young wife. To be sure you told the old woman just what she wanted to know. All the same," he went on in his puzzled way—"all the same, I *can't* see just why it should be a tadpole that has first no legs, then two legs, then four. I've puzzled it out and I've puzzled it out, and still I can't understand. I just can't understand."

Sadko the Minstrel

RETOLD BY CHARLES DOWNING
Illustrated by ROBERT J. LEE

IN THE glorious town of Novgorod there once lived a minstrel named Sadko. He possessed but little gold, and to earn money he went round the noble feasts and banquets and enchanted everyone—princes, boyars, and merchants alike—with his marvellous skill on the gusly, the Russian psaltery. One day, however, misfortune befell him, for no one that day summoned him to play at any feast or banquet. Then a second and a third day passed, and still the minstrel Sadko remained without hire, and sighing deeply, he went down to the shores of Lake Ilmen, sat in the shade of a rock and began to pluck the strings of his maple-wood gusly. He played thus all day, and just as evening was falling, the waves of the lake suddenly swirled and roared and the waters were clouded with sand.

Sadko was terrified, and running away from the lake, he returned to the town of Novgorod.

The dark night passed and the light of day came again, but still no one invited Sadko to play at a feast, and finding his enforced idleness most tedious, the minstrel went again down to the shores of Lake Ilmen, sat in the shade of the burning rock, and began to play. He played all day, and as dusk fell, the waves of the lake suddenly swirled and roared and the waters were clouded with sand, and Sadko ran away and returned to Novgorod. And still on the third day no one invited Sadko to a feast, and again he went down to the shores of Lake Ilmen and played all day in the shade of the burning rock. And as dusk fell on the third evening, the waves of

117

the lake suddenly swirled and roared and the waters were clouded with sand. This time, however, Sadko was not afraid, and he continued to pluck the strings of the psaltery on the shore of the lake. And then, when he had played thus for some time, the waves of the lake suddenly swirled and roared louder than ever, and before the terrified minstrel could move a limb, the waters parted, and out of the lake stepped the mighty figure of the great King of the Blue Seas!

"We thank you, Sadko of Novgorod," roared the King, "for you have greatly diverted us. I have held a great banquet in this Lake of Ilmen, and you have enchanted the ears of my guests with your playing, and all are grateful to you. I know not, Sadko, how rightly to reward you for your services, but go now, return to Novgorod, and tomorrow you shall be summoned to play at a banquet given by a rich merchant. All the rich men of Novgorod will be present, and when they have eaten and drunk their fill, they will all begin to praise themselves and boast. One will boast of his immense wealth, one of his excellent steed, another of his strength and valour, and another of his youth. The wise will boast of his aged father and mother, and the fool will boast of his fair young wife. And you also, Sadko, shall make your boast. In the presence of all the rich merchants you must say: 'I, Sadko the Minstrel, know that in Lake Ilmen there are fish with fins of pure gold!' The rich merchants of Novgorod will laugh and contradict you and say that there are no such fish in Lake Ilmen, whereupon you must make a wager with them. Wager your turbulent head against their shops and precious wares, and when they accept, take a silken net and come and cast it into the lake three times, and each time I shall send you a fish with golden fins. In this way you will win row upon row of shops in the market and you, Sadko the Minstrel, will become one of the richest merchants of Novgorod."

Sadko returned to Novgorod, and lo and behold! on the next day he was invited to a great banquet given by a rich merchant. Everything happened as the King of the Blue Seas had predicted. When all the rich merchants had eaten and drunk their fill, they began to boast of their achievements. The one boasted of his countless treasure, the other of his strength and valour, the wise man boasted of his aged father and mother, and the fool of his fair young wife, and all the while Sadko sat and said nothing. When the rich merchants had finished their boasts, they turned to the silent minstrel and asked him whether he had nothing to boast about, and laying aside his gusly, Sadko said: "Alas, merchants of Novgorod, what should the poor Sadko have that he could match his boasts against yours? I have no countless golden treasure, and I have no fair young wife. I have only one thing whereof to boast, for I alone know that in Lake Ilmen there are fish with fins of gold!"

At this the merchants of Novgorod burst out laughing and argued with him, saying there was no such fish in the lake.

"If I were rich," cried the minstrel, "I should wager a great sum on the truth of what I say. As it is, I have nothing but my own turbulent head to stake."

"We shall accept your wager, Sadko!"

laughed the merchants. "We say there are no fish with golden fins in Lake Ilmen, and we wager all our shops in the market and all their precious wares against your turbulent head!"

Hereupon Sadko took a silken net, and going down to the shores of Lake Ilmen, cast it into the waters. He cast it once, and straightway drew out a tiny fish with golden fins. A second time and a third time he cast in his net, and each time he drew out a tiny fish with golden fins. The merchants of Novgorod were amazed, but seeing there was nothing to be done and that the minstrel had spoken true, they gave him their shops in the market with all their precious wares, and Sadko the Minstrel became one of the richest merchants in the glorious town of Novgorod, and began to trade. And he journeyed from place to place and to many towns of Russia near and far, and when he had made great profits, he took a fair young wife, and built himself a palace of white stone, and as the red sun, the bright moon, and the silver stars shone in the heavens, so did a sun, a moon, and a host of silver stars shine in the halls of Sadko's palace, for he adorned it with all things of beauty. Then Sadko organized a great banquet and invited to his palace all the rulers and merchants of Novgorod to take part. The governors Luka Zinoviev and Foma Nazariev were there with all the freemen of the town, and sitting down to the feast, they ate and drank their fill, and began to boast their boasts. Then Sadko rose to his feet, and walking through the magnificent halls of his white palace, he addressed his guests thus:

"Powerful lords, rich merchants, and freemen of this glorious town of Novgorod! You are all welcome guests at my banquet. You have eaten and drunk and grown merry, and you have filled your bellies and boasted your boasts. What should I, Sadko, now boast of? My golden treasure is inexhaustible, my flowered robes will never wear out, and my trusty druzhina is incorruptible. I will therefore boast a mighty boast! I wager that my wealth is so great that I can buy up all the wares, good and bad, for sale in the glorious town of Novgorod!"

Then Foma Nazariev and Luka Zinoviev stood up on their sturdy legs.

"Sadko, rich merchant of Novgorod," they said, "how much do you wager?"

"Rulers of Novgorod," replied Sadko, "what would you that I wager of all my countless treasure?"

"Let your wager be thirty thousand roubles."

So Sadko the Merchant wagered thirty thousand roubles and the banquet came to an end.

When Sadko awoke the following morning, he roused his trusty druzhina, gave them as much gold as they could carry, and going down to the market, he bought up all the goods of Novgorod, both good and bad. A second and a third day he did the same until not a single thing of Novgorod remained for sale. As soon as the wares of Novgorod itself were exhausted, however, the fine wares of Moscow arrived to fill the market, and Sadko began to reflect on his folly.

"How could I boast to buy up all the wares for sale in the glorious town of Novgorod?" he said. "Even if I buy up all the wares that now arrive from Moscow, more will arrive from beyond the seas, and how should I, Sadko, buy up all the wares of the wide, white world? Glorious Novgorod is richer than I, and it is better to pay the thirty thousand roubles I wagered than to fritter away all my riches in a fruitless task."

Thus did Sadko lose his great wager against the wealth of Novgorod, and surrendering the thirty thousand roubles, he built thirty black boats, loaded them with all the wares of Novgorod and sailed away to sell them in the wide, white world. He sailed from Novgorod to the Volkhov, thence to Lake Ladoga, from Lake Ladoga to the River Neva, and from the River Neva into the deep, blue sea. And sailing to the lands of the Golden Horde, he sold there the wares of Novgorod, and filling his casks with red gold, his barrels with pure silver, and many coffers with fair round pearls, he sailed back across the sea in the direction of Novgorod. But when the ship was in the middle of the ocean, the

winds howled, the waves beat, and the sails tore from the masts until the black ships could move no more, and Sadko summoned his faithful crew.

"My good and faithful crew," he cried. "We have journeyed far across the sea, but never yet have we paid tribute to the great King of the Blue Seas. And now he threatens us with storms and demands his due. Hurry, take a cask of red gold and cast it into the blue sea!"

And they took a cask of red gold and cast it into the blue sea. But still the winds howled, the waves beat, and the sails tore from the masts, and the ships could not move. Then Sadko ordered a barrel of pure silver to be cast into the blue sea, and after that a coffer of fair round pearls, but still the cold winds howled, the great waves dashed, and the sails tore, and the black ships could make no headway across the face of the ocean.

"Alas, my brave crew!" cried Sadko, "it is clear that all the treasure we pos-

sess will not suffice as tribute to the great King of the Blue Seas. He demands a human life and that alone will pacify him. Let each one of you make a counter of lead, and writing his name upon it, cast it into the blue sea. I, your captain, will make mine of red gold, and whosoever's counter sinks to the bottom of the ocean shall follow as tribute to the mighty King of the Blue Seas."

And when they threw their counters on to the surface of the sea, all the lead ones bobbed and floated like ducks on a lake, but Sadko's golden counter sank straight to the bottom.

"These lots are not fair!" cried Sadko. "Let everyone make counters of red gold, and I, your captain, shall make mine of oak!"

But when they cast the counters into the sea, all the golden ones floated on the surface, while Sadko's oaken counter sank straight to the bottom. And though Sadko commanded the crew to make their counters of oak while he made his of lime, still it was his counter that sank to the bottom of the sea.

"Alas!" sighed Sadko. "There is nothing to be done! It is I that the King of the Blue Seas desires. Come, my good crew, bring me my merchant's ink-well, my swan's quill, and pen and paper bearing my seal."

And when his men had done as he commanded, Sadko sat on his folding chair at his oaken table and wrote his will. And sharing his possessions among the Holy Church, his younger brothers, his young wife, and his brave and trusty crew, he began to weep.

"Come, my brave and faithful crew," he said. "Place an oaken plank on the blue sea that I may cling to it, for thus shall I find death less terrible."

And taking his maplewood gusly, he bade farewell to his native town of Novgorod, descended onto the oaken plank on the surface of the waters, and watched the black ships move away; and left alone in the middle of the ocean, he fell asleep.

When Sadko awoke, he found himself on the very bottom of the deep ocean. The red sun shone brightly through the clear water, and there in front of his eyes stood a great palace of white stone, and when he went in, he beheld the mighty King of the Blue Seas seated on his coral throne.

"Welcome, Sadko of Novgorod, rich merchant and minstrel!" cried the King. "You sailed a goodly time on the face of the ocean without paying tribute to its King! However, now you have come in person to pay me tribute, and since you are a great master on the gusly, I would bid you play me something now."

Sadko took his maple gusly and struck up a merry tune, and the King of the Blue Seas began to dance. And as he danced the whole ocean trembled, the waves on the surface dashed together, and many black ships sank to the floor of the ocean with much treasure and many good true believers who died praying to Mikola Mozhaiski to save them from the cruel sea. As he was playing, Sadko felt a hand on his right shoulder, and turning his head, he saw behind him a small, white-haired old man.

"You play well, Sadko of Novgorod," he said. "These are gay tunes for the Kingdom of the Blue Seas."

"Alas, batiushka," said Sadko, "I would

fain play a sad song, for I have no freedom in the blue sea, and it is the King who bids me play for him."

"If you wish to escape, Sadko," replied the old man, "I can help you."

And thereupon the old man whispered in the minstrel's ready ear what he had to do to escape from the watery domain in which he now found himself.

"And when you return to Holy Russia," concluded the old man, "build there a cathedral in the name of Mikola Mozhaiski, for I am he."

And having said this, the old man disappeared and Sadko was left alone. Thus, remembering what Mikola had told him to do, Sadko broke both the strings and pegs of his psaltery, the music ceased, and the mighty King of the Blue Seas could dance no more.

"Why do you play no more, Sadko?" asked the King.

"The strings of my gusly have snapped, Your Majesty," replied the minstrel, "and the pegs have come apart."

"Ah, well," sighed the King. "I suppose it cannot be helped. You have already afforded me much pleasure, and I should like to make you happy in the Kingdom of the Blue Seas. Would you not like to marry one of our beautiful sea-maidens and settle for eternity here?"

"I bow to your will, Your Majesty," replied Sadko, for Mikola Mozhaiski had told him it would be perilous to refuse.

"Very well," said the King. "Tomorrow you shall choose for yourself a bride who shall be your equal in wit and reason."

All came to pass as Mikola Mozhaiski had said. A great parade of all the eligible sea-maidens of the Kingdom of the Blue Seas was held on the following day, and although Sadko was much struck by their beauty, he kept his passions in check, and suffering the first three hundred maidens to pass by, and then the second three hundred, he finally chose the last maiden of the third three hundred, a dark and beautiful maiden named Chernava, just as Mikola had told him to do. The King of the Blue Seas then gave a great banquet to celebrate the marriage, and when the time came for Sadko to retire with his new wife, he remembered the old man's warning that if he touched her at all, he would never see his motherland again. So, forbearing to kiss or embrace his bride, Sadko dropped off into a deep sleep, and when he awoke, he found himself back on dry land on the outskirts of Novgorod, and there, sailing along the River Volkhov, came his own black ships with his good and faithful crew. Joyously Sadko ran to meet them, and when they saw him waving from the high banks of the River Volkhov, his men were amazed, for they knew that they had left their master to die in the middle of the blue ocean, and here he was in Novgorod before them! They rejoiced greatly to see him and embraced him, and all went together to Sadko's white-stone palace where he kissed his young wife and related all that had happened to him. Then Sadko unloaded his ships of their countless golden treasure, and with it he built one great cathedral church in the name of Mikola Mozhaiski and another to the glory of the Blessed Mother of God, and praying to God to forgive his sins, Sadko sailed no more out into the blue sea, but spent the rest of his life peacefully in his native town of Novgorod, beloved and praised by all.

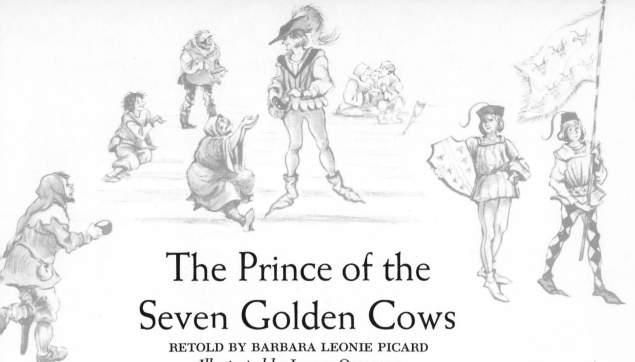

The Prince of the Seven Golden Cows

RETOLD BY BARBARA LEONIE PICARD
Illustrated by LILIAN OBLIGADO

A LONG TIME ago there lived in a town in Gascony a prince who had for his coat of arms seven golden cows, and from this he was known as the Prince of the Seven Golden Cows. He was very rich, and of all men in Gascony he was the most generous. Every morning of his life he went to hear Mass, and on leaving the church he would find all the beggars and the poor of the town awaiting him on the church steps, and to each one of them he would give liberally, day after day, so that they would call to heaven to witness his charity and declare, "Prince of the Seven Golden Cows, there is no one like you in all the world. For your sake we would go through fire and water."

Every evening of his life he would feast with his friends: the noblemen and the well-to-do merchants of the town. At his tables were good food and good Gascon wine in abundance, and no guest ever left his castle without a fine gift to carry home; so that they would call to heaven to witness his splendour and his bounty

and declare, "Prince of the Seven Golden Cows, there is no one like you in all the world. For your sake we would go through fire and water."

One day a young man came to the castle and asked to speak with the Prince. He said, "I have heard of your kindness and I am come to beg a favour. There is surely in all this town no one more unfortunate than I. When I was seven years old, my father and my mother died, and since that day I have worked hard to earn my keep. For a few happy months I have been betrothed to a maiden, as good as she was lovely, and we were soon to have married. But this morning she died, and I think that I shall never be happy again. If I knew enough Latin to read the prayers in the prayer book, I would become a monk, but I know no Latin. Have pity on me, Prince of the Seven Golden Cows, and give me fifteen crowns to buy mourning."

"My friend," said the Prince of the Seven Golden Cows, "I am indeed sorry

123

for you. You shall have not fifteen, but one hundred crowns, and may you meet with no more misfortunes."

The young man thanked the Prince of the Seven Golden Cows and went, taking with him the hundred crowns. But after three days he returned, wearing mourning. "Prince of the Seven Golden Cows," he said, "you have been kind to me. There is nothing else for me to live for. Let me be your servant and dwell in your castle, and I will serve you faithfully and ask no wage."

"I would not ask any man's service without paying him his hire," said the Prince. "But if that is as you wish it, it shall be so."

In that manner the young man became a servant in the castle of the Prince of the Seven Golden Cows, and so well he worked and so loyal he showed himself, that the Prince set him over all his other servants. But always the young man wore mourning, so that he came to be known as the Black Steward.

One day he came to the Prince of the Seven Golden Cows. "Lord," he said, "you spend too much on your guests, and you give too much in charity. Within a year your coffers will be empty of gold and silver, and you will be ruined."

"What does that matter?" asked the Prince of the Seven Golden Cows. "I have neither wife nor child to be my heir. I shall spend my gold until it is gone. And when that day comes, I shall still be rich enough, for I have many good friends who will not see me want. Time after time have they told me that for my sake they would go through fire and water."

"You cannot be certain of that," said the Black Steward.

That evening, as they feasted, the Prince of the Seven Golden Cows said to his guests, "Often have you all said to me that you would go through fire and water for my sake, yet today the Black Steward has told me that I cannot be sure of it. How do you answer him, my friends?"

And they one and all cried out against the Black Steward, calling him a rogue. "He steals from you and he cheats you and he cannot be trusted," they said.

The Prince of the Seven Golden Cows sent for the Black Steward. "My friends have called you a thief who steals from his master. Tell me, Black Steward, are they speaking the truth?"

The Black Steward denied nothing. "It is true. I have stolen from you, lord."

In anger the Prince of the Seven Golden Cows drove the Black Steward from his castle, bidding him begone forever. And the Black Steward, who had indeed robbed his master of enough gold to buy a castle, went far from the town to where the River Gers flowed slowly and sleepily past the meadows and vineyards of Gascony; and there, on the bank of the river, he bought a castle and the land around it, and in the castle he waited for what he knew would come to pass.

When a year was all but gone, the Prince of the Seven Golden Cows saw that his coffers were empty and knew that he was ruined. He gave a last banquet for his guests; and when the feasting was over, he said, "My friends, my coffers are all empty and my gold and my silver are spent, and I have nothing left to offer you. So many times have you said to me that for my sake you would go through fire and water. Now that I am ruined, give me your help."

But his guests looked at one another, and their looks were dark, and they scowled. "Prince of the Seven Golden Cows," they said, "you have wasted your wealth in alms-giving. Go, ask the poor for help, not us."

The Prince of the Seven Golden Cows could hardly believe he had heard aright; but when he saw how they turned their backs on him and spoke amongst themselves as though he were not there, he knew that he was not mistaken. He went out to the poor and the beggars, and they called to him for alms. "My friends," he said, "I can give you nothing, for I have nothing left to give. My coffers are all empty and my gold and my silver are spent. But so many times have you told me that for my sake you would go through fire and water that I have no

fears for the future. You are poor, my friends, and you have little, yet will you not share that little with me?"

But the beggars all cried out against him, saying, "You have squandered your wealth in food and wine and in feasting with your guests. Why should we share with you the little we have? Go, beg your bread, even as we do."

The Prince of the Seven Golden Cows could hardly believe he had heard aright; but when he saw how the beggars muttered together, cursing him and shaking their fists because he had nothing to give them, he knew that he was not mistaken.

He stood sadly in his courtyard, crushed between the scorn of his guests and the blame of the poor; and then there came a great clattering of hoofs from the street outside and the baying of many hounds, and into the courtyard rode the Black Steward, a big cudgel in his hands

and a pack of huge hounds at his horse's heels.

"After them! Away with them!" cried the Black Steward to the hounds; and they ran, biting and snarling, among the beggars and the noblemen and the well-to-do merchants, whilst the Black Steward himself laid about him with his cudgel, until the courtyard was clear. Then he dismounted and went to where his master stood. "Lord," he said, "they were ungrateful, so I have driven them away."

But the Prince of the Seven Golden Cows looked coldly at the Black Steward. "I ask no services from one who has robbed me," he said.

"Lord, I robbed you that there might be something left to you when you were ruined. On the bank of the River Gers there stands a castle which awaits the arrival of its lord. It is yours."

So the Prince of the Seven Golden Cows left the town forever and went to live in the castle on the quiet bank of the Gers, and there the Black Steward served him without wages, even as he had done in the old days. And so things went on for seven years.

Then, on the last evening of the seventh year, the Prince of the Seven Golden Cows sent for the Black Steward. "In all my life," he said, "I have found but one loyal friend, and that is you. I would tell you my great secret, that you may profit from it when I am gone. Seven years ago, when my coffers were empty and I had spent all my gold and silver on the giving of alms to those who were thankless, and on the feasting of those I believed my friends, I could, had I wished, have gained more riches to replace all I had lost. Yet this I did not do,

because I had at last learnt the ingratitude of all men save myself. But now I am growing old, and within a year I shall be dead. I would wish you, my only friend, to be my heir, so I will tell you the secret of the Seven Golden Cows which are the device of my house. First, fetch an axe, then saddle two horses, and we shall ride forth together."

The Black Steward fetched an axe and saddled two horses, and he and the Prince of the Seven Golden Cows rode out of the castle into the winter's evening. At midnight they reached a cross-roads, close by a marsh where many weeds grew.

"Take your axe," said the Prince of the Seven Golden Cows to the Black Steward, "and cut the tallest of the reeds. But take care, for the reed will seek to protect itself, and it will change its shape three times whilst you are cutting it. Three times only may you strike with your axe, and if by the third stroke you have not cut the reed, you will die in that instant."

The Black Steward took his axe, and going to the tallest of the reeds, he grasped it firmly and raised the axe. At once the reed changed into a serpent with seven hissing heads. But the Black Steward struck boldly, for all the fearsome sight. When he raised his axe for the second stroke, he saw how the reed had become a new-born child. For a moment only he hesitated, then he struck boldly. As he raised his axe for the third stroke, the reed took the likeness of his long-dead betrothed, and the Black Steward trembled and the axe almost dropped from his hand. But he remembered the warning of the Prince of the Seven Golden Cows, and he summoned up all his strength and his courage, and he struck boldly for the last time. And in his left hand he held the tallest of the reeds, severed at the root. He returned to his master.

"You have done well," said the Prince of the Seven Golden Cows. "Now cut from the reed enough to make a flute." When this was done, they returned to the castle.

For the next five months, every night, when the servants of the castle slept, the Prince of the Seven Golden Cows taught the Black Steward a certain tune to play on the flute. And when mid-June was come, and the eve of St. John, the Prince said, "At midnight, bring two cauldrons, six leathern sacks, and the flute, and come with me to the meadow by the river."

At midnight, with the flute, the cauldrons, and the sacks, they stood on the bank of the Gers. "Now play on the flute the tune which I taught you," said the Prince of the Seven Golden Cows.

The Black Steward did as he was bidden, and at once the ground opened, and out of the earth came seven golden cows. They bowed their heads before the Prince and waited. "Milk the cows into the cauldrons," he ordered. So the Black Steward milked the cows into the cauldrons until the cauldrons were full; and the milk of the seven golden cows was golden coins.

"Now fill the sacks with the gold," said the Prince. When it was done, the Prince of the Seven Golden Cows showed the Black Steward a certain spot in the river. "Throw the sacks into the water," he said. As the last sack sank under the water, it was dawn, and the earth opened and the golden cows disappeared.

A month later, the Prince of the Seven Golden Cows was dead, even as he had said. The Black Steward saw him buried with all the splendour fitting to his rank, and then he went to the castle in the town where the Prince had spent his wealth in feasting his guests and in giving alms, and from there he had the news cried about the streets that the Prince of the Seven Golden Cows was dead, and that he had died rich.

At once the noblemen and the well-to-do merchants and the beggars flocked to the castle. "How sad the news! The good Prince of the Seven Golden Cows, there was no one like him in all the world. For his sake we would have gone through fire and water. Perhaps he has remembered us in his will," they said as they crowded into the courtyard.

Then the door of the castle opened and the Black Steward rode forth, his big cudgel in his hands and his hounds at his horse's heels. "After them! Away with them!" he cried to the hounds. And the hounds ran, biting and snarling, among the noblemen and the merchants and the beggars, whilst the Black Steward laid about him with his cudgel until the courtyard was empty. "Let that be the legacy of the Prince of the Seven Golden Cows," he said.

Then the Black Steward returned to the place where the Prince of the Seven Golden Cows was buried, and he studied and learnt Latin. And when he knew enough Latin to read the prayers in the prayer book, he became a monk; and with the gold from the River Gers he built a monastery, where night and day he prayed for the soul of his master, the Prince of the Seven Golden Cows.

The Water-Sprite and the Bear

RETOLD BY BARBARA LEONIE PICARD

Illustrated by LILIAN OBLIGADO

IN A MILL beside a stream, a short way from a village, lived a miller. He was a cheerful, good-natured man, and would have been contented enough with his lot had it not been for one misfortune. In the stream close by the mill lived a water-sprite, a sly, ugly creature with dank hair like water-weeds, sharp, pointed teeth and flat, webbed feet.

At first it was bad enough when the water-sprite's head would suddenly appear above the water and he would look inquisitively as anyone passed by; but it was worse when he began to climb on to the bank of the stream and sit there, showing his long teeth in a thoughtful grin and watching with his unblinking, pebble-like eyes the miller or his wife, the serving-wench or the boy who helped in the mill.

"He gives me the creeps," said the miller's wife, "sitting there like that."

And the boy said, "He is ugly, and no mistake." But the serving-wench just gave a scream whenever she caught sight of him, picked up her skirts and ran.

Yet all that was nothing to what came later. The miller had had little to grumble about so far. But one day the water-sprite padded up the steps to the mill, put his head round the door, said, "Good morning, miller," in his wet voice and came in and settled himself comfortably on the floor in a corner by the hearth.

The miller was not one to grudge a warm, dry corner to anyone, not even to a water-sprite—the last kind of creature, surely, whom one would expect to want such a thing—but the water-sprite took to coming into the mill whenever it pleased him, at any hour of the day or night, and prowling around for all the world as though it were his own place,

129

so that, just when one least expected him, there he would be: under the table at supper time, waiting in the kitchen the first thing in the morning, padding behind one on his silent feet when one had supposed oneself to be alone, or appearing suddenly at a dark turn of the stairs just as one was going to bed. Or perhaps the very worst of all was when, after an evening in which he had—most happily—failed to appear at all, he would be found curled up asleep in the middle of the bed, lying on a patch of damp bedclothes, for, of course, he always dripped stream water wherever he went.

In a few weeks he was quite at home in the mill, and one could be sure of meeting him there at least once every day. By this time the serving-wench had left—running all the way home to the village one night after finding the water-sprite on the stairs in the dark—and her place had been taken by no fewer than three others, each of whom had, in turn, quickly followed her example, and the miller's wife was having to do all her own work.

One evening, the water-sprite showed great interest while the miller's wife was cooking the supper, coming quite close

and sniffing at the roasting meat. The next morning he arrived at breakfast time, carrying a fish on the end of a stick. He sat himself down by the hearth and broiled his fish over the fire. When it was cooked, he tasted it cautiously, liked what he tasted and ate it up in two bites. After that he always cooked his meals at the hearth, four or five fish at breakfast and supper, and scrunched them up, heads and tails and bones and all, with his long teeth, watching the miller and his wife thoughtfully as he did so, in a manner which they found most disconcerting. It quite put them off their own meals.

Another pretty trick of his was to set the mill wheel racing in the middle of the night, so that the miller and his wife would wake up in a fright, and the miller would have to get up and go to see what was the matter.

It was, of course, inevitable, with such a state of affairs, that there should come a day when the miller found himself alone in the mill. Not a single girl from the village would come to work for him, his boy's father had found the lad another master, and his wife had gone home to her mother. So the miller was all alone—all alone, that is, save for the water-sprite. But because the mill was his livelihood and had been his home as well for all his life, he had to stay on, in company with the water-sprite; and little comfort he found in such a companion.

One evening, just after dark, a bear-ward knocked on the door of the mill and asked lodging for the night. He was on his way from one village to another with his dancing bear. The miller sighed, for he dearly liked a good evening's talk and he saw little enough of other folk these days, and the bearward looked a cheerful fellow with a merry grin and a bright eye, a man, indeed, after the miller's own heart.

"It is unlike me to be inhospitable," said the miller. "Not so long ago I never dreamt there would come a day when I would turn a stranger from my door at night. The village is only a few miles on, my friend, you had best go there, to the inn." And he told the bearward about the water-sprite. "It is all I can do, to stay here myself," he said. "A hundred times a week I tell myself, 'Tomorrow I shall lock the door and throw the key in the stream and go.' But I always manage just one day more. Yet one cannot expect a stranger to put up with it."

"I am not afraid of a water-sprite," said the bearward with a chuckle. "But I have walked a long way today, and I have no mind to walk even a few miles more. I am tired, and so is Braun here." He jerked a thumb over his shoulder towards the shaggy brown bear on the end of a chain.

"Very well," said the miller, "come in, and most welcome you will be. But never say I did not warn you." He stood aside to let the bearward through. "You had best bring your bear in with you; you never know what may happen to him if you leave him in the barn."

The bearward laughed. "Braun can take care of himself. He would make short work of any water-sprite, I warrant. Just you let us have a sight of this plague of yours and we may be able to do you a service, Braun and I."

The water-sprite had already had his supper and gone back to the stream, so the two men had a pleasant evening together, chatting of this and that, and since the water-sprite did not appear again before they went to bed, to the miller it seemed quite like old times, and he began to feel more cheerful than he had felt for months.

The miller and his guest shared the big bedroom, with the bear curled up on the floor beside the bed; and there was no sign of the water-sprite all night.

They got up early in the morning and went down to the kitchen for their breakfast, the bear coming after them. But, early as they were, the water-sprite was earlier. There he was, sitting by the hearth, the embers raked together to make a good fire for him to cook his breakfast on, and four broiled fishes laid out on the floor beside him in a row, ready for him to eat when he had cooked the fifth.

The miller's face fell, and the morning suddenly seemed not so bright and pleasant after all. "There he is," he whispered miserably.

The water-sprite looked up, showed his teeth and, "Good morning, miller," he said. He gave one glance at the stranger, saw nothing to interest him there, and went on with the cooking of his last fish.

The bearward watched him for a moment; then he turned to the miller, winked, and called back over his shoulder, "Come on, Braun, here is your breakfast for you. Look, good fish." He pointed, gave the bear a push, and the bear ambled towards the hearth, sniffed at the fishes laid out on the floor, liked what it smelt, picked one up and swallowed it in one bite—one bite more quickly than the water-sprite could have managed. Before the water-sprite realized what was happening, the bear had taken a second helping; but before it could manage a third, the water-sprite had jumped to his feet, quite furious, and was shaking his fists at the bear. "Away with you! Away with you, you thieving creature!"

The bear sat up and looked at the water-sprite, but made no attempt to go away. Instead, after a moment, it made a move to take the third fish.

"My fish! My fish!" screamed the water-sprite, beside himself with rage. And he rushed at the bear to drive it away.

The bear put out a great paw and clouted the water-sprite, who shrieked and turned tail, making for the mill door and his stream as fast as he could, followed by the growling bear. At the door the bear turned and came back for the remaining three fishes, which it ate happily by the fire, while the miller, delighted with the way things had turned out, made the breakfast.

The bearward laughed loudly. "Well," he said, "did I or did I not tell you that Braun would make short work of any water-sprite?"

After breakfast the bearward went on his way to the village and the miller began his work, feeling happier than he had felt for a very long time. In fact, he felt so happy that he sang at his work, a thing he had long forgotten to do.

All that day the water-sprite never showed himself near the mill, and it was the same the next day, and the next, for nearly a week; and the miller was feel-

ing on top of the world and thinking of taking a day off from work the very next morning and going over to his wife's mother's house to tell his wife to come home, when, coming whistling into the kitchen for supper, he saw the water-sprite sitting by the hearth cooking his fish.

The miller could have wept. Now it would start all over again, he thought. No wife, no boy to help him, no serving-wench, no peace in the mill, ever again.

"Good evening, miller," said the water-sprite, showing his long teeth. But the miller had not even the heart to give him a civil answer—though he usually did, just in case the water-sprite took offence: one never knew, and it was al-

ways best to be on the safe side, with those long teeth.

The miller sat down at the table, too miserable to trouble about getting himself any supper. After a time the water-sprite said, "That big cat of yours with the long claws, miller; I have not seen it for several days. Has it gone away?"

For a moment the miller went on staring at the table top, thinking regretfully of the bear, not even finding the idea of a bear-sized cat amusing, though it would once have made him laugh. Then suddenly his heart gave a great bound, for he was really quite a quick-witted man. He looked up and said, as casually as he could, "Why no! She has just had kittens. You will be seeing her around

again soon, and all the seven little ones with her. They are just like their mother, only smaller. But they will soon grow. They will soon grow."

The water-sprite looked at the miller with his round, pebbly eyes even rounder than usual, if that were possible. Then he dropped the fish he was cooking and sprang up. "Is that so? Seven little ones?" he said with a shriek. "Then I am off! Good-bye, miller, you will not be seeing me again." And he was away out of the mill as fast as his flat feet could carry him, and into the water and down the stream and away for good and all.

And the miller never set eyes on him again.

The Man with the Bag

From The Big Tree of Bunlahy

BY PADRAIC COLUM
Illustrated by ROBERT J. LEE

ONCE UPON a time a man who had a beggar's bag on his back came to the door of a house that was hereabouts. He asked for shelter. "And if you let me take my rest here while I'm begging through the parish, I'll ask you for nothing else, ma'am," said he to the woman of the house. "A good beggar doesn't ask for food where he gets shelter and doesn't ask for shelter where he gets food. I know what a good beggar's conduct should be. My father was a beggar and his father was a beggar before him. I'm no upstart."

The woman of the house told him he could rest by the fire when he finished his round of begging in the evening.

When she told him this, the man with the bag on his back turned from the door and went along the crooked lane that went from the house.

The woman's daughter was there, and she looked after him as he went down the laneway. She thought that only for the grime that was on him and the ragged clothes that he wore he would be good-looking enough.

Let the beggarman go on while I tell you about the girl. She was named Liban, and well did she deserve the name which means "Beauty of Woman," for her eyes were beaming, her mouth was smiling, her cheeks were like roses, and her hair was brown as a cluster of nuts. But for all her beauty Liban had little chance of being wedded.

Young men came to ask for her in marriage, but if they did, her mother told them they were first to climb the tree that overhung the high cliff. There they would find a raven's nest, and from it they must take a pair of scissors that the raven had carried off. They must also bring back two of the raven's eggs. One young man and another young man would climb the tree. But when he came to the top branches that overhung the cliff and found them breaking under him, he would get down from the tree and not go to the house again.

So Liban stayed, and was likely to stay, beside her mother's hearth, spinning threads on her spindle while her mother spun them upon her wheel. And this was just what her mother wanted her to be doing, for she got a deal of silver for all the thread that she and Liban spun.

The beggarman came back in the evening and his bag hung as if there were nothing in it. All the same, he refused the cup of milk and the cut of bread that Liban offered him. "All that I'll take in your house," said he, speaking to her mother, "is the place to rest myself, and leave to put in your charge what I get on my travels."

And saying that, he put his hand down into the bag, and searched and searched there, and brought up what he found. It was a pea. "I'll leave this in your charge and you'll be accountable for it," said he. "I'll take it back from you when I'm going."

She took the pea and put it on the corner of her spinning wheel. Then the beg-

garman put the bag under his head and went to sleep by the fire.

Liban and her mother came out of the sleeping room at the peep of day, and as they did the beggarman got up from where he was lying. He opened the house door, and went off on his rounds with the crooked lanes of the parish before him. Liban went to get ready the breakfast. The little speckled hen that was her own came in to pick up the crumbs that would be around the table. But when she came as far as the spinning wheel she saw the pea, and when she saw it she picked it and swallowed it.

"Mother," Liban said, "the pea that the beggarman left in your charge, my own little speckled hen has swallowed."

"He'll forget to ask about it," said her mother. "As for you, take the spindle and get some threads down while the breakfast porridge is cooling."

The first thing the beggarman said when he came in the doorway was, "Where is the pea I left in your charge, woman of the house?"

"A hen ate it."

"Which is the hen that ate the pea I left in your charge?"

"The speckled hen that's before you."

"If the speckled hen ate the pea that was mine, the hen herself is mine."

"That cannot be."

"It can be and it is, ma'am. It's the law, and if a beggarman doesn't know the law, who would know it?"

And saying this he took up the hen that was picking from a dish on the floor and put her into his empty bag. The woman of the house believed what he said, for she had once stood in a court—the Court of Dusty Feet it was

—and had heard a sentence passed on a man who had lost something that was left in his charge and that he was accountable for.

When he was going off the next morning, he took the speckled hen out of his bag. "I leave her in your charge," he said to Liban's mother.

Then he went off, facing the crooked lanes of the parish, his empty bag hanging on his back. And Liban, so that nothing might happen to her, made a little pen of wattles for the speckled hen, and tied her inside of it. Then she took up her spindle, and her mother went to her wheel. "I wish that beggarman had come to ask for you in marriage so that I might have made him climb the tree," she said.

Liban was looking out of the door. She saw the pig beside the pen of wattles. The pen was strange to the pig, and she went rooting around it. The speckled hen flew into her mouth. The pig ate her. All that was left of the little speckled hen was the white feathers on the pig's snout.

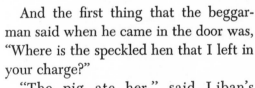

And the first thing that the beggarman said when he came in the door was, "Where is the speckled hen that I left in your charge?"

"The pig ate her," said Liban's mother.

"Then the pig is mine. That's the law, and if a beggarman doesn't know the law, who'd know it?" He went out to the yard and took the pig by the leg and dragged her into the house. He put her into his bag and tied up the mouth of his bag. Then he went to sleep by the fire.

By the time the beggarman went out of her door next morning, Liban's mother had lost so much flesh through grief at the loss of her pig that she looked as if the weight of a pig had been taken out of her. She wasn't able

to eat her porridge either. Liban took charge of the pig. She tied her to a bush under a wall of loose stones, thinking no harm could come to her there. Then she went back to her spinning. But before she had more than a few threads spun, a horse galloping toward the house threw the stones of the wall down upon the pig.

"Every misfortune has come on us since that beggarman came to the house for shelter," said the mother. "He'll want to take our horse now. If he does and rides away on him, I'll be content with my loss, so glad I'll be to see the last of the beggarman."

He came back in the evening with a corner of his bag filled. "Where's my pig?"

"Our horse has killed her."

"Your horse is mine."

"Take him and ride away, and may all my bad luck go with you."

"No. I never stay less than five days in any house. It's due to a promise I made to my father. He feared that I might become a vagabond, one day here and another day there, and he made me promise I'd stay the greater part of the week in any house I had been given shelter in. One day more I'll stay for the sake of the promise I made. Mind the horse for me. I put him in your charge."

He lay by the fire, his head on his bag, and he went to sleep. The next morning he went off, his bag on his back, and his face toward the crooked lanes of the parish. Liban put a halter on the horse and, so as not to let him get into any danger, went with him everywhere the horse went to graze. Along the cliff he went where the grass was sweetest. When they came to the tree that the raven's nest was in, Liban put her hands before her eyes so that she might look up and see how high the young men had to climb when they had asked for her. Not so high at all, she thought. And there was the raven on the branch above the nest, flapping its wings at her. As she looked, the horse, leaning out to get a mouthful of sweet grass, slipped and slithered down the cliff. And the raven with a croak flew down after him.

So poor Liban went back to her mother. "Our horse is gone now," she said. "Over the cliff he has fallen, and what will the beggarman take from us now?"

"Nothing at all can he take," said her mother. "Let him take the horse's skin, and come near us no more."

When he came back that evening with only a corner of his bag filled, the beggarman said, "Where's my horse so that I can go riding tomorrow?"

"The horse fell over a cliff and the raven is upon him now."

"Who was minding my horse when he fell over the cliff?"

"My daughter was minding your horse."

"Then your daughter is mine. That's the law, and if you don't think it is the law I'll stand face to face with you about it in the Court of Dusty Feet."

Saying this the beggarman lifted up Liban (and, oh, but his arms were strong!) and thrust her into his bag. Then he put the bag on his back and ran from the house with her.

Her mother ran after him. The neighbors ran with the mother. But the beggarman's legs were long and strong and his back was broad and unbending. "Liban's in the bag, Liban's in the bag! Stop him! Stop him!" cried her mother and the neighbors. But their cries only made him go faster and faster. When he came to the crossroads he laid the bag upon a bank, and he let Liban come out of it.

"Take me back to my mother," said Liban.

"Indeed, I'll do nothing of the kind," said the man. Now that he had taken off his ragged coat and had washed his face in the stream, he looked a handsome sort of a young man. "Here's a coach," he said. "It's waiting for you and me, and we'll go in it, not to the Court of Dusty Feet, but to the court in my father's castle where there will be one who will marry us. I put on the beggar's garb and carried this bag upon my back only to come to you, Liban, Beauty of Woman. There are many things I can do, but there are a few I can't do, and climbing a tree is one of them."

Then he put his arm around her and lifted her into the coach that was waiting there, with two black horses to draw it. They had just got into the coach when Liban's mother and the neighbors came up. The neighbors stopped to pick up the shower of silver that the coachman threw them, and the footman lifted Liban's mother and left her standing on the board beside him, and the coach went dashing on.

138

The Good Housewife and Her Night Helpers

RETOLD BY BARBARA KER WILSON
Illustrated by ROBERT J. LEE

IN DAYS gone by, thrifty housewives used to spin their wool and weave their cloth late at night, when they had finished their daytime work. This was the custom of Inary, the wife of a prosperous farmer who lived on Tiree, hard by a fair green mound called Burg Hill, which was known as a faery dwelling-place.

On a certain night as she sat spinning by candlelight after her husband and the rest of the household had gone off to bed, a great tiredness came upon Inary, and putting her hand to her brow she exclaimed aloud:

"Oh that someone would come from land or sea, from far or near, to help me with the work of making this cloth!"

She had no sooner spoken than she heard a knocking on the door, and a chanting voice called to her:

"Inary, good housewife, open the door to me; for I am come to help you in your work."

Wonderingly Inary arose and opened the door; and there on the threshold was a strange wee slip of a woman dressed all in green. She entered the room and went straight to the spinning-wheel, where she began to ply the shuttle without further ado. Inary had no sooner shut the door behind her when there came a louder knocking, and another sing-song voice called out:

"Inary, good housewife, open your door; for I am come to help you in your work."

And when Inary unlatched the door for the second time, another weird green woman came into the room, and took her place at the distaff.

But this was by no means the end of it, for hard on the heels of the second stranger came a third green woman, and then a fourth, a fifth, a sixth, and a seventh: until at last poor Inary lost all count of her visitors, and stood in helpless amazement, watching as they settled down with extraordinary eagerness to carding and teasing her wool; plying her weaving-shuttle quick and fast; thrumming her loom with restless fingers; and busily boiling the fulling-water that was used to clean and thicken her homespun cloth.

"Surely it is all the faeries of Burg Hill who have come to my house this night!" she said to herself.

There was now such a din and clatter in the place, with the green-clad, dark-skinned little women jostling one another for elbow room, that it was a great wonder the good man who slept in the adjoining room was not awakened. Yet in spite of all, he slumbered with uncanny soundness through the uproar, and Inary began to fear that the little people had put spells on him. Meanwhile, her shrill-voiced helpers continually cried that they were hungry, and she endeavoured to get enough food prepared for them. And if she was tired before they came to do her work, she was now seven times as tired with trying to keep their mouths filled. As the night advanced, their enormous appetite seemed to keep pace with the fantastic speed of their labours; and it appeared that the universe itself could not keep them in meat and bread. By midnight, Inary was ready to drop down from her toiling, and her one thought was how she might rid herself of her faery visitors. It was in vain that she went into the adjoining room to try to wake her husband; she might as well have striven to rouse a millstone, for no matter how loudly she shouted in his ear, he did not stir.

When she was almost at her wit's end, she thought of going for advice to a certain wise man who lived near by. Leaving the green-clad ones eating her last baking of bread, with only a little bannock left toasting on the hearth, she slipped away and took the path to the old man's cottage, where she poured out all her trouble to him and implored his help.

"How can I get rid of the wee folk?" she asked him, "and how can I waken my good man, who sleeps as though he is under spells?"

The wise man chid her for her thoughtlessness in ever having asked for uncanny help from land or sea, from far or near, in the first place, and said:

"So long as you live, do not again wish, ask, or pray for that which you may regret having brought upon yourself. You are right in supposing your husband to be under spells; and before he can be awakened, your faery visitors must be got out of the house, and part of the fulling-water sprinkled over him. And the way you shall get rid of the wee folk is this:

"You must return to your house and, standing by the open door, cry out three times, as loud as you can: 'Burg Hill is on fire!' The green company will then leave their work and rush out to see if this is so. As soon as they are outside, you must shut the door and then set to and disarrange, reverse, overturn, and upset all the implements with which they have been working. The rest will look after itself."

Thanking the old man for his good advice, Inary hastened back to her house. Reaching the open door, she cried out with all the strength she could muster:

"There is fire in Burg Hill! Burg Hill is on fire! Burg Hill is in red flames of fire!"

Before she had finished uttering the third warning, out from the house rushed all the faery folk with one accord, crushing and trampling one another in their anxiety to be away. And as they went, each one of them cried for the things she held most dear, which lay in the faery hill:

> *"My husband and little ones,*
> *My cheese and butter-keg,*
> *My sons and daughters,*
> *My big meal chests,*
> *My comb and wool-cards,*
> *Thread and distaff,*
> *Cow and fetter,*
> *Horses and traces,*
> *Harrows and board,*
> *And the ground bursting,*
> *My hammers and anvil,*
> *Burg Hill is on fire,*
> *And if Burg Hill is burnt,*
> *My pleasant occupations*
> *And merriments are gone."*

As soon as Inary saw that they were all out of the house, she went in quickly and shut the door. Then, as she had been told to do, she deranged everything with which the faeries had been working. She took the band off the spinning-wheel, twisted the distaff the opposite way, turned the loom topsy-turvy, and took the fulling-water off the fire. She had barely finished doing this when the faery company, having found out how she had tricked them into leaving the house, returned and knocked at the door, the blows of their knuckles coming as thick and fast as hail-stones in winter.

"Inary, good housewife, let us in!" they cried.

"I will not," she replied.

So they called to the spinning-wheel to let them in.

"Good Spinning-wheel, get up and open the door for us."

"How can I," said the Spinning-wheel, "when I am without a band?"

They now appealed to the distaff.

"Good Distaff, open the door for us."

"I would willingly do so," replied the Distaff, "but I am twisted contrary."

Then they thought of the weaving-loom.

"Good Weaving-loom, open the door for us."

"That I would do with pleasure, but I am turned topsy-turvy," it answered them.

There was yet the fulling-water to call upon.

"Good Fulling-water, will you not open the door?"

"I cannot, when I am off the fire," said the fulling-water.

The little folk were getting exhausted and impatient, and as a last resource they turned and besought the little bannock that was toasting on the hearth.

"Little Bannock of good fortune, open the door quickly!"

The Little Bannock jumped up and hopped to the door as fast as it could; but the good housewife was quicker yet. She ran after it and nipped it with her hands, so that it fell with a plop on the floor.

When they realized that there was indeed no way for them to enter the house, the faeries began shrieking and crying until their hubbub became unbearable.

Then at last Inary remembered what she had to do with the fulling-water, and taking a panful into the next room, she threw it over the good man, who awoke immediately. And high time it was too. As soon as he heard the terrible noise going on outside, he rose up from his bed, flung open the door of the house, and stood on the threshold with a black frown on his face.

And immediately the uproar ceased and the wee folk faded away like green shadows, never to trouble Inary again.

"*Count Beet*" *is a most unusual fairy tale.*
It is a story in which the chief character is an earth spirit
who tries to understand
the world of men and falls in love with a human princess.
Another peculiar thing about this story is
that our sympathy is not
with the abducted princess but with the unhappy gnome—
it is hard to decide whether he is a mistaken hero
or a defeated villain.
Written especially for this collection,
the story is a free adaptation of an old German folk tale.
It is the first time this version has appeared in print.

Count Beet

RETOLD BY LOUIS UNTERMEYER
Illustrated by ROBERT J. LEE

MILLIONS and millions of years ago, deep down in the earth under a huge mountain, there lived an elemental and powerful gnome. The world was still new; it had not yet cooled off; there was nothing on it but barren land and steaming water. Every ten thousand years or so, the gnome would come up and look over the slowly changing world. It did not interest him very much, and there were not many changes during ten thousand years. He was the lord of a vast subterranean kingdom; he had countless slaves to do his bidding and work wonders for him. Still, he was curious about what was happening—or going to happen—on the surface of the earth. More than a million years passed before there was any sign of change; many more millions before

things began to grow, to come to life, crawl out of the great seas, learn to walk, to leap, and even to fly.

Ages were added to ages, and then one day the gnome saw a new world. He saw men. He watched them, wondering, while they built houses, made fires, tamed animals, sowed seeds, harvested crops, and raised families.

"That must be a fine way to live," thought the gnome. "I must try it. I must learn what these creatures are like, how they live, and how they think."

Disguising himself as a plowman, he applied for work to a rich landowner. Everything he did went well, for the soil obeyed him. The crops grew rapidly, and he was considered the best worker in the village. But the landowner was a spendthrift; he never had money for his workers and barely paid them enough to keep them from starvation.

The gnome refused to work for an employer who cheated him, so he hired himself out as a shepherd to the land-owner's neighbor. He took excellent care of the flock. He guarded the ewes and lambs better than they had ever been cared for; he found places where there were sweet grasses and health-giving plants. Not one sheep fell from the cliffs; no single lamb was torn by a wolf. But his employer was a miser. He refused to give the shepherd his rightful share. On the contrary, he claimed that several of the sheep had been lost, and he deducted their value from the shepherd's wages.

Cheated for the second time, the gnome thought more carefully what sort of man he should work for next. He decided to enter an honored profession and, as a law student, became clerk to a judge. Soon, however, the transformed gnome found out that the judge was not only unrighteous but actually dishonest, that he paid no attention to the laws, was hard on the poor but was always ready to do favors for the rich. When the clerk refused to carry out one of the judge's cruel orders he was put in jail. It was, however, an easy matter for the gnome to escape. He merely changed into a breath of air and wafted himself through the keyhole.

Disappointed and disillusioned, he sank back into the depths of the earth. His first experience with men had been unhappy and he resolved to have nothing more to do with them. He marvelled that Mother Nature permitted such creatures to exist, and could even be kind to them.

Yet he continued to be curious and, after staying underground many, many years, he resolved once more to try to understand the human race.

This time he was more cautious. He did not join people at their work, but watched them from a safe distance. He hid himself on the edge of dark forests, peered at them from behind bushes, and drifted noiselessly through valleys and little villages.

Then, one day he happened to spy a group of girls. One of them was the loveliest thing his eyes had ever seen, so young and beautiful that he could not believe her to be one of the daughters of men. She was a king's daughter, be-trothed to the knight, Roland, and she and her six companions often went into the woods to pick wild strawberries, mushrooms, and rare flowers which she brought back to the castle. In the warm weather she loved to linger in the cool shadows of the trees and, when the days were hot with summer, bathe in a pool beneath a waterfall.

This was one of those days. The gnome, who had often observed the princess and her six companions, re-mained hidden as the group came to the pool. He heard their low voices change to cries of delight and astonishment. The pool was there, but everything about it had changed. The rough boulders were now smooth marble and gleaming agate. The water no longer gushed wildly from a hole in the rocks; instead, it trickled gently down steps of carved stones like a miniature waterfall, making an ex-quisite music as it fell into a twenty-foot bowl of alabaster. The pebbly bottom had been turned into gold and silver sands, and from four directions came four soft breezes, each one carrying a different perfume. Daisies, buttercups, and pale blue forget-me-nots embroidered the border of the pool; wild jasmine, hedge-roses, and honeysuckle made a living curtain, and every bush held a shower of many-colored blooms. There were niches in the marble background, and these contained delicious cakes and sweetmeats in dishes made of ivory; crystal goblets glistened with cooling drinks. A path of sparkling mica and mosaic pictures led to the pool where the water flickered with all the colors of the rainbow.

Overcome with surprise, the girls stared, clapped their hands, and cried out their pleasure. Then, laughing in a dozen keys, they leaped into the pool. Playfully they swam about—until the princess gave a sudden shriek and sank out of sight. The other girls dived after her, but all they caught was a glimmer of golden hair. They saw a whirlpool forming at the bottom of the pool with an opening like an endless funnel, and down this the princess disappeared.

There was nothing left to do but to inform her father, the king. As they drew near the castle, they met him returning from a hunt. After he had learned what had happened, his grief could not be controlled. He tore his clothes, buried his face in his purple mantle, and groaned: "My lost darling, my lovely Lora—I am the most miserable of men. I will not rest until she is found." Then suddenly he cried out, "What am I doing? Why are we staying here? Take me to the spot and show me that treacherously enchanted place!"

But when they came to the pool, it was as wild as it was before it had been transformed. The water tumbled through raw rocks. There was not a trace of marble or agate or alabaster, there were no forget-me-nots, no roses, no bowers of jasmine and honeysuckle. A cold wind rattled dry branches. Sick at heart, the king turned back to the castle, and the girls followed sadly.

Meanwhile, Lora was safe in the gnome's kingdom. She did not know how long she had been asleep nor who had worked a magic spell; when she woke she had no idea where she was. She reclined on a luxurious sofa covered in rose-colored satin with a ruffle of sky-blue silk. A young man stood before her, and in this guise the gnome told her about his mysterious origin, his powers, his possessions, and his desire that she should be his bride. Saying that he had built this palace for her, he led her through huge halls, magnificent chambers, and richly decorated rooms. He showed her a pleasure garden with summer-houses, terraces, and grassy turf as smooth as a dance floor. In the center of the garden stood a fountain that spread itself into opening and folding fans of spray or shot up into a thin spire of dazzling diamonds. There were strange trees that shed continually changing shadows, and each tree bore a new and different kind of fruit. There were peaches sprinkled with flecks of silver; there were apples that were purple on one side and pink on the other; there were nectarines with skins of gold, cool and crisp to the taste. Each tree housed a hundred birds, and when they sang their many-toned voices made a symphony sweeter than anything ever heard on earth.

In spite of all these wonders, the princess shuddered at the thought of marrying the gnome. She grew listless and melancholy. She barely glanced at the beautiful things, but sighed deeply and disconsolately. The gnome did everything he could to divert and please her, but it was useless. Finally he thought of a plan. Human beings, he said to himself, are like bees and ants; they need company. If she had her own kind to talk to, to entertain and play with, she would be happy.

He did not hesitate another moment. He went into the field and dug up six large beets, put them in a basket, and brought them to the lovely Lora, who was sitting sad-eyed in a rose-shaded arbor.

"Put all gloomy thoughts out of your mind," he said, "and open your heart to joy. In this basket is everything you need to make you happy here. Take this striped little wand, wave it gently in the air, and these earth-grown things will turn to any earthly creatures you desire." And with these words he left the princess.

The moment he was out of sight, she opened the basket and waved the magic wand over it. "Bella! Bertha! Brenda! Bona! Bryna! Brynnhilde!" she cried. And before the wand stopped waving, Lora's six companions stood before her. They cried out, kissed and clasped her, and she kissed and embraced each one in turn. Lora could not tell whether she had summoned her playmates from their places on earth or whether she had really changed the six vegetables into her six playmates. But she was too happy to trouble her mind about it. All she cared about was that she had company, the company she loved best. She showed the girls the garden, made them taste the silver peaches and the golden nectarines, took them through all the rooms of the gnome's palace, and displayed all the treasures. They admired the gowns made of the finest tissues and the richest velvets, wound the moonbeam-sheer scarves around their shoulders, put the necklaces and enamelled lockets about their throats, and tried on every jewelled ring, brooch, bracelet, diadem, and earring.

The gnome, who had spied upon them, was delighted with what he had done. "Now," he reflected, "I am beginning to understand the nature of mankind—and womankind. All you have to do to make them happy is give them what they want."

He noticed that Lora looked more amiably upon him; she smiled whenever they met. She was truly a princess again, for she was surrounded by her court-maidens, and no queen was ever better served.

For a while everything was perfect. The gnome's kingdom was transformed by a flurry of laughing girls. There were songs, dances, and the sound of stringed instruments from morning to night. Then one day Lora noticed that Bella was looking pale. When she looked closely at the others, she saw that Bertha seemed tired, Brenda's full color was fading, Bona could not dance, Bryna's quick laughter ceased, and Brynnhilde was always asking to be excused from play. When Lora inquired if anything had happened to displease them, they assured her that nothing was wrong. Yet, though the princess thought up new amusements and the gnome supplied them with every delicacy for their delight, the six maidens grew thinner day by day. They lost their high spirits and their youth; their whole personalities changed.

One sunny morning, after a worried sleep, the princess thought of a way to bring her handmaidens back to their former selves. But as she entered the reception room, she was terrified. She saw, to her horror, six old women hobbling about on crutches, coughing and groaning, unable to hold themselves erect. Shuddering, she ran from the room to the portals of the palace and commanded the gnome to appear. When, at her first outcry, he came, she stamped her foot in rage and screamed at him: "You hideous creature! Why have you robbed me of the only pleasure I have in life here! Why did you bewitch my six carefree companions! Do you want me to go mad in this forsaken place! Give me back my girls and my happiness at once, or you'll have nothing from me but scorn and hatred!"

"Mistress," replied the gnome, "do not be angry. Everything in my power is yours to command—you have only to ask—but do not expect me to do the impossible. Nature is kind to me and will let me change some of her features, but only if I do not try to break her first law, the law of life. As long as strength and sap were in the beets, the magic wand could transform them into other things that had strength and vitality. But when the life-giving element dwindles and dies, whatever shape it has assumed must also die. Do not grieve. Another basketful of beets will undo the harm, and you can summon all the faces and figures you desire. Give Nature's wornout gifts back to Nature, and try again. In the large field beyond the garden you will find lively company." And with these words the gnome again disappeared.

As soon as he was out of sight, Lora seized the striped wand and waved it over the withered old crones. Nothing happened. So, with a shrug, she did what children do who have no further use for a broken toy—she threw the shriveled vegetables out with the rest of the rubbish.

With a light heart she ran quickly over the greensward to pick up the basket and fill it again, but it was nowhere to be found. She raced back and forth across the garden without discovering a sign of it. At the edge of the grape arbor she saw the gnome, very disturbed. Ignoring his embarrassment, she said, "You have cheated me again! Where have you hidden the basket? I've been searching for it more than an hour!"

"Mistress," he answered humbly, "please forgive my thoughtlessness. I promised more than I could perform. I've looked everywhere, but the harvest has been gathered, the crops have been stripped, the root vegetables have been dug up, and all the beets have been stored in dark cellars. The fields lie fallow, for the growing season is over. It is winter, and only your presence makes it seem like spring. Your warm heart keeps the ice from forming, and flowers grow to greet you wherever your foot touches the ground. Wait three months and you will be able to play with as many smiling and dancing dolls as you please."

Lora did not thank him for his advice. Before he finished she turned her back on him, walked away without a word, and shut herself in her room. He, however, went to a market-town within his kingdom and sent her, as a peace offering, a velvet-gray donkey laden with all manner of gay silks, brilliant brocades, and glowing satins, so that the beast and his burden looked as though they had come straight from the sunny Orient. Moreover, he gave orders to plow the fields, to plant seeds, and build an underground fire so that the seeds would develop roots and grow as rapidly as in a greenhouse.

Soon the beets began to put forth little shoots and promised an early crop. Lora watched the progress of their growth more eagerly than if she were waiting for the ripening of the golden apples of the Hesperides. But discontent clouded her cornflower-blue eyes. Restlessly she wandered among dark trees, and her tears softened the cold ground as she thought of Roland, the young knight she was to have married. Then one dusky evening that showed promise of winter's ending, she thought of a plan.

Spring came back to the mountain kingdom deep in the earth. The gnome let the underground fires die; and there, before any flower had dared to blossom, was a magnificent, full-grown field of beets. Lora, who rejoiced in the quick growth, was now ready to try her experiment. She dug up a small beet, waved the magic wand, and changed the beet into a bee.

"Fly away, little messenger," she said, "fly to Roland, who is mourning for me, and tell him that his Lora is still alive. Tell him that she is held captive by a powerful gnome, but she is planning a way to escape. Whisper this in his ear and bring back word. Then I will tell him more."

The bee buzzed his understanding of the message and flew straight from Lora's finger. But his flight had scarcely begun when a greedy swallow caught him and gulped him down. Lora saw the unfortunate mishap, but she did not grieve more than a moment.

She took another beet and changed it into a cricket. Giving the same directions, she said, "Hop off, little one. You are too small to be seen threading your way through the dark subterranean passages. When you come to Roland, tell him to be ready to rescue me."

Obedient to her command, the cricket hopped away. But a sharp-eyed, long-legged stork spotted the little chirper and, with a sudden snap of his bill, swallowed him whole.

This second misfortune disappointed Lora, but it did not discourage her. "All good things come in threes," she said to herself, and changed the third beet into a magpie. "Spread your wings, you lively chatterer," she commanded the bird, after repeating the instructions, "until you come to Roland. Tell him exactly where I am, and everything else you have heard from me. Then tell him to have men and horses waiting at the very edge of the hole leading down into the earth and be ready to carry me off should I be pursued."

The clever black and white bird

whistled sharply, rose into the air, and soared through one twisting passage after another. Lora watched him anxiously until his shining tail and white-patched wings were out of sight.

Meanwhile, Roland continued to grieve for his lost sweetheart. The coming of spring did not cheer him; on the contrary, it made him still more doleful. He wandered through the woods, ignored the bright-colored wildflowers, sat under heavy oak trees and sighed "Lora!" The woods echoed the sad syllables: "Lora! Lora! For Lora! Forlorn!" Suddenly he realized that it was not an echo he heard but another voice. He started up in amazement, and saw the magpie hopping from bough to bough.

"Unhappy chatterbox," said Roland, "who taught you to utter the name which makes this listener so sorrowful?" Picking up a stone, he cried angrily, "If I hear it once more you will not live to say it again." At that moment, the magpie spoke. "Hold your hand! Lora sent me!" And the bird related everything he had learned to the last word.

The moment Roland the knight heard these tidings his soul leaped with joy; the death-like melancholy which had settled on his spirit vanished. Eagerly he asked for more details; but the bird, clever though magpies are, could only repeat the lesson Lora had taught him. He said it once more and flew away. Roland rushed back to his residence, summoned his retainers and, with a squadron of horsemen, rode off to the mountain fastness.

Next morning, shortly after dawn, Lora appeared attired like a bride. Her dress, of the purest whitest satin, shone as if it were woven with moonbeams; a necklace of fire-opals burned about her neck; her head was crowned with a diadem of a hundred gems, and ropes of pearls were twisted in the braids of her golden hair. "Yes," she said softly to the astonished gnome, "I am now ready to become the queen of your kingdom. But first I must ask you for one more proof of your desire to please me. I must know the number—the exact amount—of beets growing in that acre. I want my marriage to be the biggest and most beautiful in the world—I will need dozens of bridesmaids to attend me, many little flower-girls; and hundreds of other witnesses. I must know *exactly* how many to be sure of, so do not deceive me. Count the beets to the last one and bring me the total—that will be the last test of your devotion."

The gnome listened eagerly. Then, without waiting to reply, he rushed off to the beet-field and began the allotted task. It was, as the sly Lora meant it to be, a long and difficult assignment, and the gnome was so anxious to complete it that he continually made mistakes. Five times he counted the beets—and got five different results. Then, more slowly and more uncertainly, he started over again.

As soon as the gnome was out of sight, Lora busied herself with her plans for flight. She had hidden a particularly large beet, and this she changed into a swift, red steed with saddle, reins, and stirrups. Quickly she swung herself upon the horse's back and rode down the dark passages, over rocks and rivers, hedges and heights, until they came to the chasm in the mountain and, without a change in pace, Lora dashed up the sides to the very top. There Roland and his men were waiting for her.

The gnome was still so occupied with his work that he saw nothing, heard nothing, and suspected nothing. Finally, after much trouble and many mistakes, he finally arrived at the correct total of all the beets, large and small, down to the last leafy sprout. Having completed the labor, he hurried happily back to claim his bride. But Lora was nowhere to be found. He ran anxiously through the meadow, peered into the flowery arbors, but there was no sign of her. He searched through the palace, looked through every room, opened every closet, but he could not find what he sought. He called "Lora! Lora!" but the only answer was the echo of her name.

Then he noticed the disorder of her room—the cupboard drawers pulled open, the clothes flung about—and he saw how he had been fooled. Casting off his bodily form the way a man throws off a coat, the gnome resumed his phantom shape and rose into the air. But when he issued from the depths of the mountain all he could see was his intended bride far in the distance, vanishing beyond his power, crossing the border of his rulership into her father's kingdom. Frantic with disappointment and trembling with rage, he reached up into the sky, clapped two black clouds together and hurled a bolt of lightning at the fleeing girl and her escort. But he was so overcome with emotion that his aim was poor and he struck only a thousand-year-old oak.

At that moment his mood changed, for his grief was far greater than his anger. He returned to the palace and went from room to room, sighing and weeping. He wandered through the great pleasure garden, but nothing in it gave him the least pleasure. He cursed himself bitterly. "It is my own fault," he cried. "What insane curiosity drove me to try to understand the ways of men and women. It is a good-looking but cruel and treacherous race, and, henceforth, I will have nothing more to do with it!"

Uttering these harsh words, he stamped violently upon the ground—stamped three times—and the palace, the pleasure garden, and all the other wonders vanished. He closed up the chasm, blocked all the passages, and, opening a path through the rocks for himself, sank deeper and deeper until he reached the center of the earth, taking with him his hurt as well as his hatred.

After Lora and Roland had reached her father's castle there was no end to the rejoicing. There were feasts and festivals, carnivals all day and fireworks at night. There was a resplendent wedding. Lora's father shared his throne with his daughter and, when the monarch died, Lora reigned as queen.

Lora never tired of relating the story of her adventures in the gnome's mountain kingdom, her clever ruse, and her bold escape. The tale grew with each retelling—it became a popular legend—and people found Lora's trickery so amusing that they called her foolish victim "The Beet-Counter." Later generations mockingly shortened it to "Count Beet." As the years passed, they even forgot that he was a gnome, an unearthly spirit who had once tried to understand human beings but, having failed, never again visited the disenchanting world of mortal men.